UNDER THE GRAVE

BOOK FOUR OF THE GRAVEDIGGERS SERIES

UNDER THE GRAVE

WILLIE E. DALTON

Hope you enjoy!

Willie

Edited by Lessa Lamb
Cover & Interior Design by We Got You Covered Book Design
www.wegotyoucoveredbookdesign.com

www.authorwilliedalton.com

If you've been reading my books for very long, you know that this book is late. Very very late. For that, you have my deepest apologies. *Under the Grave* was written during a more challenging phase in my life, between exhaustion and delays, on my part and others, it took forever to bring it all together. I hope that the story itself makes up for the time it took to get it to you. And always, thank you for reading.

Love,
Willie

"So," he asked. "How's death?"

"Hard," she said. "It just keeps going."

— Neil Gaiman, *American Gods*

CHAPTER
ONE

THE GRAY SKYLINE I ONCE FOUND SO DREARY WAS now alive with subtleties I would have never seen without my chartreuse vampire eyes. I marveled at the swirls and patterns painted through the bleakness. The dirt was darker and richer now, not just to my eyes, but the smell was more potent and brimming with the scents of life and death. I could read the dirt and pick up clues about the person in each plot just from the scent of the earth. It was almost like tasting wine, or coffee. I could smell the iron, the peat, the decayed trees, and animals. Underneath was the soul's essence.

I'd reaped mechanics that smelled like axle grease, and bakers who smelled like yeast and fresh bread. Children made the dirt smell like baby powder, and people who had died violently smelled like lead, and blood.

Soren and Billy had adapted well to my transition into vampirism. They didn't say much about the change in my appearance, and asked very little about my hunting trips. I didn't mind that they weren't terribly intrigued. They had never been fond of vampires, so allowing me to live and work with them was a huge step.

However, whenever I mentioned the things I could smell in the dirt and they made the connections with the people I dug up… that seemed to freak them out just a little.

I smiled as I pushed my shovel down into the brown earth. My heart no longer ached for Raphael, and the anger I had held onto about my own murder had dissipated.

If I went into the city, I saw friends: vampires, humans, and even a god or two. Here, in the fields of the dead, I had a friend, a lover, and a useful job that I adored.

The shovel hit the small pocket of air beneath the dirt that told me I was close to the body. Gently, I scraped away the earth and looked down at the woman dressed in a bright pink suit, a pink ribbon pinned to her lapel. I didn't have to wonder at her cause of death.

I clicked on my flashlight and her eyes opened. She blinked at me a time or two and I helped her sit up.

"Hi," I said to her, trying not to startle her.

"Hmmph," she grumbled. "Is this heaven or hell?"

"Neither. Just the mixed population of the underworld," I explained.

"I'll be damned. Guess I was wrong, I thought for sure there was nothing after death." She smoothed her short mahogany brown hair and held out her hand for me to help her stand.

I helped her up. "You'll have to go into the city to get assigned. That means see how much time you have, get a job, place to live… all of those things."

"Can I get a drink somewhere? I haven't had a drink in ages. The doctors wouldn't let me drink while I was getting chemo treatments." She dusted off her suit and rolled her eyes. "That was just stupid. I was terminal when they found it—why deny me one of my only pleasures when I was going to die anyway?"

I smiled at her; I couldn't help it. I loved spunky people.

She looked at me as if she had just seen me, and furrowed her brow, "What is wrong with your eyes?"

"I'm a vampire," I told her plainly.

"Huh," she mused. "Can I get that drink?"

I did, in fact, take her for a drink before we went to the Assignment Hall. I sipped my usual, a gin and tonic, and she drank three amaretto sours before I finished my one.

She told me her name was Linette, and that she'd been a good wife to a good husband, raised her kids, and about the time she was ready to live for herself, she was diagnosed with terminal breast cancer. She shrugged, "Don't wait to do the things on your bucket list."

After our drinks I dropped her at the door of the Assignment Hall and wished her the best on her new journey.

I thought about stopping in to see my dad, Ray, or seeing Grace and Andreas, but I had other things in mind. Linette's "live for the moment" speech had inspired me, even though I was already dead.

Back in the fields I saw what I was looking for. His white t-shirt was stretched tight across his wide chest and thick arms. His pants were dirty and worn from so many hours of work. His beard added to the hard working, ultra-Viking sex appeal. And those eyes—those steel gray eyes that could make me melt with warmth and desire, or freeze me out with their utter coldness...

"Soren!" I called out to him as I approached.

He looked up at me and leaned on his shovel. "Yes?" he inquired, with a raised eyebrow.

I kept my face stern and moved towards him with purpose. "I need something from you," I said, and motioned for him to follow me as I walked past.

Without hesitation or question, he dropped his tools and followed me.

I opened the door to my little house and didn't turn around when I heard him come in behind me.

"Is everything OK?" he asked.

"Close the door," I ordered, then added, "and strip."

I heard him softly chuckle, "Ah, that's what this is: what you would describe as a 'booty call.'"

I was trying to maintain my serious, slightly dominating vibe, but that did it—hearing Soren refer to himself as my "booty call" was more than I could handle. I laughed, and felt my mood shift like a sudden change in the wind.

"I suppose you are my booty call," I said, still laughing. I was somehow feeling a little less sure of myself now. I had planned to make him strip and then jump on top of him, playing the aggressor that I so rarely was.

He walked in front of me, and now he was the serious one. His eyes locked on mine and didn't falter, even as his hands moved down to grab the hem of his shirt so he could pull it over his head.

I saw his muscles flex beneath his skin as the shirt

moved up, and then off of his body. I caught myself biting my lip, and then my eyes broke the focus as I watched him slowly unbutton his pants. He wasn't just trying to get his clothes off hurriedly to get me in bed—men were never this graceful unless they wanted to be. Soren was putting on a show for me: he was *stripping*. *My own Viking stripper*, I thought, and almost giggled again.

"What's funny, little girl?" he asked, and suddenly his eyes were burning holes into mine once more.

My plan had taken an unexpected turn. I felt my face heat up and knew I was blushing. "Nothing," I whispered.

He was naked now and moving towards me. My mouth was suddenly very dry, but I was willing to bet that lower areas weren't.

He put his large hand around my throat, and I immediately tried to swallow against the tension. I gasped in short, shallow breaths, and then his mouth was on mine and his grip relaxed.

I breathed deeply and swallowed, even as his tongue was against mine and his teeth bit at my bottom lip.

"Oh, Soren," I sighed, sinking in against his body.

"What do you want?" he asked, as he so often did.

I knew the question was asking whether I wanted him to continue to be rough, or play nice. Not being able to decide this time, I settled on, "I just want to be close."

Soren smiled and kissed me on the nose. He helped me out of my own clothes, and then sat down in my comfy reading chair.

The chair wasn't particularly wide, and the arms seemed like they would be in the way. "How is this going to work?" I asked.

Soren motioned with a finger for me come over and sit on his lap facing away from him.

"I wanted to be facing you," I started to argue.

"Just try it," he urged.

So I slowly sat in his lap as he used his hand to help guide himself inside of me. I tried to find the right angle to start moving, but he stopped me.

"Just be still a moment, feel me inside of you," he pulled me back into his arms and I closed my eyes. His hands squeezed my breasts, causing my body to tighten around him, and he moaned.

One of his hands went all the way down to tease between my legs, while his other hand found my throat once more. I sighed and melted back against him as I felt my pleasure growing. I could feel his beard against my neck as he whispered in my ear.

"My sweet, Hel. So beautiful, so strong, so fucking powerful, and so soft," he breathed as his hand worked faster.

Our hips rocked as his hand moved, and I tightened myself around him over and over again. His own grip on my throat tightened as I came, and my scream caught in my throat just behind his hand. I went limp from the intensity of the orgasm, and Soren wrapped both his arms around my torso and lifted me up and down as he thrust deep and hard until he found his own release. I screamed then, enough for both of us.

I collapsed back against him as he grew soft, still inside of me.

"Was that close enough?" he asked.

I nuzzled my face into neck. "Mmhm," was all I could say.

CHAPTER
TWO

SOREN HAD GONE BACK OUTSIDE TO THE FIELDS, and I headed to the Vampire Quarter. I needed to go above-ground to feed. I didn't like going alone, but luckily I knew that one of my other fanged friends would join me.

I strolled the black brick streets and gazed in shop windows. Before I "turned," I had thought that all of the stores always looked closed because they were so shadowed and dark, just like everything in the Quarter. Now I knew that vampire eyes were so powerful they just didn't need all of the extra, blinding, glaring lights that humans did. I could see almost everything in the store just by taking a casual glance in the windows.

Other vampires passed me and I knew most of them, though I couldn't say I had made any new friends in this part of the city. I didn't feel as out of place as I once did, though it was hard to say if that was because I was a vampire now, or just that I had spent too much time here.

I knew either Grace or Andreas should be home, and the other would be at work. I didn't really care who I hunted with, just that I ate. The more physical

7

the activity, the more frequently you needed living blood. Digging was very physical, and I had a lot of vigorous sex with Soren... so it seemed like I was *always* needing to eat.

My hand was almost on the lion's head door knocker when the door abruptly swung open. I quickly stepped back and saw that it was Boude stepping out.

His long red curls hung over one shoulder and I could see he had part of his hair pulled back on top. We smiled when we saw each other.

"Looking for a hunting partner?" he asked.

"I am. Do I look like I'm starving?" I replied.

He laughed. "Just an educated guess. Shall we go to my place?"

"Sure, but should we invite Andreas?" I asked.

"He just returned from his own meal and is sleeping. I just came to drop off a pair of Grace's boots that I found," he said.

"Is she here?" I asked without thinking.

His demeanor gave away only the slightest hint of discomfort. "No, she's at Melinoe's."

Grace was my best friend, and Boude's girlfriend up until very recently. She met Melinoe (the daughter of Hades and Persephone, and the goddess of ghosts and nightmares), and they had taken a strong liking to one another, causing her to end her relationship with Boude.

I tried not to let Boude see my regret in asking; no one wanted pity, especially not a vampire. "I see," I said.

Boude forced a smile, and I followed him down the streets to the alleyway where his place was tucked away.

He was dressed in green and gold, two of his favorite colors that he knew he looked good in. His emerald eyes and fiery hair sparkled and shimmered even in the dimmest of light.

Boude and Andreas were so fun to look at, and even though I was a vampire now as well, I still just wanted to sit and pet them like pretty little dolls.

Apparently I had been staring at Boude since we entered his apartment.

"Is there something wrong with my face?" he asked.

"Not at all," I said, trying to blink my vision clear and refocus. "Just admiring your beauty—and I think I really need to eat," I laughed.

He chuckled, "You know, you are very striking yourself, but you were even before you turned."

"Thank you," I said. To some, that would have seemed like flirting, but Boude and I had enjoyed our time as lovers, and that was the past. We were friends now—good friends—and I was glad we could still appreciate one another.

"Living room or bedroom?" he asked.

"Living room," I answered. "If we went to the bedroom, I'd fall asleep when we got back, and I need to get back to the fields."

He nodded.

Boude let me take the couch, and he took the loveseat. We both laid down, and within moments we were walking around unfamiliar streets at night in the world of the living. My ears were filled with the sounds of loud music, and laughter.

People stumbled out of the bars smiling, holding on to one another for support. Drunk people were always so easy.

We made our way into a dark bar, where jazz music blared, and the smell of liquor that filled the air was only slightly less overwhelming to the senses than the sugary sweet scent of cotton-candy-blood awaiting me. Women everywhere were eyeing Boude and trying to discern if we were together.

I winked at him, and he returned it with his still striking, but now human-looking, eye. I made my way to the bar and sat down.

The bar was packed, and I was lucky to find a stool. I knew the bartender wouldn't notice me for a while, but that was OK. I wasn't here to drink alcohol. In the underworld, I could eat or drink whatever I wanted, but in the world of the living, blood was all we could have.

"Can I buy you a drink?" a voice asked.

I turned on my stool and smiled, surprised to see a guy standing beside me that was much younger than I was used to. I resisted the urge to ask him if he was old enough to buy me a drink.

I could have let it play out: let him buy me a drink that I would pretend to sip, as he threw back drink after drink, until I was certain he wouldn't remember what happened afterwards. However, I was anxious to get back to the fields, and I was hungry. I was too tired for games, fun as they might be.

"Actually, I was really looking for company more than a drink," I said, and gave him a smile big enough to match my bold words. Being a vampire had certainly made me more direct, but then again, I wasn't actually trying to seduce this guy. He was just dinner.

The guy grinned and ducked his head a bit. He was blonde, but not like Soren. He was clean cut, and most certainly early twenties. He wore a salmon colored polo shirt and jeans that were torn at the factory before he bought them. He was cute, but really not my type.

"I can definitely give you some company," he said.

I jumped down off my seat and inclined my head towards the door. "Shall we?"

"Right behind you, babe," he said, his voice thick with desire.

I gave Boude a casual nod where I saw him leaned against the wall talking with two women draping themselves across him.

Outside, the guy followed me down the street and into an abandoned alley.

"Is this where you're parked, or do you live nearby?" he asked.

I heard a trace of concern in his voice, so when I responded I made my own voice a little breathier. "No, I just don't want to wait another minute," I said, turning to face him.

All worry was gone as he came up to me and started to kiss me. I turned my head and kissed a soft line down the side of his throat before sinking my fangs into his flesh.

He gasped and all his muscles tightened for a split second, then he relaxed into my arms and I held him between my body and a wall until I had my fill. He would be fine; all he would remember was making out with some strange woman right before she left him in an alley.

Boude had done the same with one of the women I'd seen him with inside. We paid a cab driver to help them into the cab and drop them at the addresses listed on their licenses.

Full and happy, we opened our eyes once more, back to the comfort and silence of Boude's living room.

CHAPTER THREE

BODY AFTER BODY, SOUL AFTER SOUL... WE HAD BEEN making up for all of the time we lost while everything was in an uproar in the underworld, when Hades opening the doors had stopped people from dying in the living world for a few days. A lot of people die every day, so even just a brief pause caused us to get very backed up once things were moving again.

Billy was digging beside me. He and Margaret were staying together almost every night now, and he was different. Not different in a bad way: he was more put together now, even when he was working. He had spent so much of his life alone, I was glad he had someone now.

Soren and Billy had both dug up souls that hadn't disappeared, so Soren offered to take them both into town to get assigned. I'm not sure if Billy or I was more surprised. Soren had definitely gotten more comfortable with going into town.

Billy was whistling, and I found myself humming along.

"Do you think you and Margaret will get married?" I asked out of the blue.

He stopped whistling and pondered my question; he didn't seem surprised that I had asked.

"I've thought about it," he said.

"Do people get married here? I mean, now that I think about it, I haven't heard of any weddings."

"If people plan to stay here, they can, or if they are moving on to the same place they might want to," he told me.

"That makes sense," I said. "You told me once before you'd like to go to heaven. Is that still your plan?"

Billy was a little quiet, and I realized I was probably being nosey.

"I'm sorry, I wasn't trying to pry—just talking," I laughed, trying to ease the weighted mood I'd created.

"No, you're fine. It's stuff I think about, but just don't really say out loud."

"You don't talk to Margaret about this sort of thing?" Now I was a little surprised.

"Not a lot. I'm afraid if we have different ideas of where we're going and what we want, that this won't last. I'd rather just enjoy it while I can." He shrugged.

"I understand that, but isn't it in the back of your mind even when you're happy?" I asked.

"A little, I guess."

"You should talk to her about it. The two of you seem to be on the same page about most things, anyway," I suggested.

"That's a good point," he agreed.

I watched as a smile crept across his face.

"What about you and Soren?"

I gave him a look that said not to go down this road.

He ignored it. "Do you think the two of you will get married?"

"Ha!" I choked. "I don't think he feels the same about marriage after his reunion with Eira—and what does forever even mean if you're already dead?"

"You're awfully pessimistic about tying the knot for someone who wants me to do it," he chuckled.

"I didn't say I wanted you to get married. I just asked if you were thinking about it."

"I left the two of you here to work!" Soren's voice grumbled as he walked up to us. "I didn't know you'd stand here and gossip." He smiled as he came over to us and kissed me on the cheek.

Billy and I ended our conversation, both feeling a little unsettled now, and resumed digging alongside Soren.

I have such a great way with words…

Hours passed and souls were reaped. Billy was the first to stop for a while, heading to his house to shower and change before going to have dinner with Margaret.

After he left, Soren turned to me. "Do you want to go into town and have dinner together?"

I kept shoveling while I said, "Sure, we can grab a bite. Let me finish this grave."

I felt Soren watching me. He walked over and put his hand on my shoulder. I stopped shoveling. "What is it?" I asked him.

"No, I mean let's get ready and go out for a nice dinner," he said.

"You mean like a fancy date?" I asked, unsure I was hearing him correctly.

He smiled. "Yes, like a fancy date."

I raised an eyebrow in suspicion. "What's brought this on?"

"Women like to be treated special. It's something we haven't done before. I mean, we go out to grab food, but not like a date." He had given this a lot of thought.

I smiled at him. My introverted Viking wanted to take me on a fancy date, and I was pretty sure great sex was going to follow. There's no way I was turning that down.

"Of course I want to go on a fancy date with you." I leaned towards him, and his lips met mine. "Would you mind finishing this grave for me? It'll take me awhile to get ready."

Soren held his hand out for the shovel. I handed it to him and winked, before practically skipping to the house.

I couldn't recall if Soren had ever seen me looking truly nice or dressed up. He'd seen me outside of work clothes, sure, but not like I wanted to look tonight.

I had a moment of near-panic, thinking there was nothing in my closet that was what I was hoping for, then I remembered a black dress that Grace and Andreas had insisted I take. It was absolutely not my usual style, much too fancy for anywhere that I would ever go. But I had seen it hanging in the boutique one day and tried it on on a whim. My friends had made such a big deal about how well it suited me, that I had kept it. Truthfully, it was even too nice for a fancy dinner. This was almost a ballroom dress—but what the hell.

I showered, and put on a full face of makeup, with smokey eyes and a nude lipstick (so Soren could still kiss me). I curled my hair, and pinned it up loosely, and then put on my dress.

It wasn't me staring back from the mirror, it was a version of myself I didn't recognize. She looked hot, though! More importantly, she looked happy.

A knock came from my front door, and then it opened. "Are you ready, love?" Soren's voice called through the small house.

I stepped out of the bathroom and walked towards the front of the house, a little nervous about him seeing me.

Soren's eyes flared with emotion, and he covered his mouth with his hand and then stroked his beard, but he said nothing.

I was taken aback myself. Soren was standing there in a dark gray suit that looked as though it had been perfectly tailored to his body. The jacket was open, and he wasn't wearing a tie, but his shiny black belt matched his shoes, and he had trimmed his beard so that is was perfectly neat.

Neither of us had spoken, we were just staring at one another.

I went to him, and he took my hands in his, looking me up and down. "My Hel, so incredibly beautiful. I just don't have the words."

I kissed him lightly, the faintest brushing of lips. "My Viking cleans up nice," I grinned, and rested my face against his neck, breathing him in.

His big hands wrapped around the sides of my waist and I sighed.

"Ya know, I'm not really hungry. We could just stay in," I suggested.

He gave a rich, warm laugh. "After all this work to get ready? I don't think so." He pulled my waist and hips towards himself even harder, and I could feel him through the slacks. He was as eager as me to get these clothes off. He cupped my face in his palm and stared into my eyes, "Let's see how long we can stand it, hmm?"

This was one challenge I didn't care if I won.

CHAPTER
FOUR

I WAS GLAD THAT I COULD STILL EAT IN THE underworld. It would have been disappointing to have only sipped a glass of blood while watching Soren eat.

There were still so many little places in the underworld that I hadn't explored, and I was somehow always surprised by everything that was available. The restaurant Soren chose was lovely. The ambience was very romantic, with low lighting and candles on the table. A large crystal chandelier hung in the center of the dining room, and the servers wore impeccable uniforms. Soft violin music played, as the artist herself strolled around the room. I was not overdressed, and Soren should have worn a tie.

I ordered herb roasted chicken and vegetables in a white wine sauce, and Soren was quite excited to find his favorite fish on the menu. We split a bottle of sauvignon blanc, and simply sat across from one another, smiling.

The meal was delicious, and I had enjoyed every bite. I was also still ready to tear off Soren's suit and have my way with him—again.

"What now?" I asked. The food had sated one hunger, and it wasn't my lust.

"Now, we go dancing," said Soren, with a grin that told me he knew exactly how sneaky he was being.

"Dancing! Really?" I asked excitedly.

Soren stood up and stepped beside my chair, holding out his hand to me.

He didn't take me far, just through the dining area of the restaurant and around the corner, into a room that was even more elegant than the one we had been in.

The dance floor was black with swirls of gold running throughout. Another large chandelier hung overhead, only this one glittered and cast shadows across the room.

A band stood on stage playing soft and easy music, while a beautiful woman with dark skin wearing a gold dress stood at the microphone. Her voice was smooth and feminine, but had that depth that most women could never achieve—it made me want to drink scotch and smoke a cigar.

Soren pulled me into his arms, and we glided across the dance floor with him leading me in every step and turn. Ray had taught me how to dance: we'd spent many afternoons in the cabin, listening to his old records and laughing as I stepped on his feet. He'd say, "Now, Hel, if you'd just let me lead, you wouldn't even have to think about what to do next."

I smiled, as I followed Soren's lead effortlessly. "Where did you learn to dance?"

He dipped me, and said, "A man must have a few secrets."

I rolled my eyes at him and kissed him.

Three women nearby caught my eye. I'd noticed

them earlier in the dining area. When I looked directly at them, they looked perfectly normal—just pretty friends, out for a night of dinner and dancing. When they were out of focus and my eyes just caught glimpses, that's when things were strange. I felt like I could see them watching me—like they were glaring at me—and in those moments, they were unsettling.

One second, they appeared to be lovely young women, with long blonde hair, in pretty dresses. The next, they were old, with thin gray hair, dressed in rags, with faces that appeared more menacing than cheerful. They reminded me of the pained expressions I had seen in Hell.

I stared at them until Soren kissed me again, and I decided that it was just the lighting playing tricks on me. I smiled at him, but it didn't quite reach my eyes.

"What's wrong, my love?" he asked.

"I think going to Hell left me with a few scars," I told him.

"I imagine it did. I know that I frequently have to pull you closer when we sleep because you have nightmares." He pulled me in against him a little more, as if that's what he was doing now.

"Really?" I asked.

He nodded. "You don't remember them when you wake up, at least not that I can tell."

"I'm glad that I can't," I shivered.

We kept dancing even closer and closer to one another, and if I pressed myself against him any harder we would have been indecent. "I've had a great time, but I kind of want to get out of here now."

"Are you surrendering to me?" Soren asked.

"Always," I grinned.

"Yes," he said with a sigh, "let's get out of here."

"I'm going to go freshen up before we leave." I kissed him again, and walked off to find the ladies room.

The restroom was as luxurious as the rest of the place, decorated in shades of rose and gold. The entryway had a large pink couch, a dressing table with an ornate mirror, and plush rug on the floor. Once inside, the sinks were golden bowls on counters of white marble, and the lighting was soft and flattering. Three stalls were in the restroom, and the doors for them went from floor to ceiling, adding privacy and that touch of class that only toilets in the finer establishments had.

I took my nude lipstick from my small clutch and leaned towards the mirror to re-apply it, as well as touch up my eyeliner—more out of habit than necessity. I had always been a fan of what eyeliner did for my eyes; now that I had the pupil-less eyes of a vampire, I liked it even more.

I was just tucking my things back inside my bag, when all three stalls opened at the same time, and out stepped the three women who had been watching me.

They were all much taller than they had appeared across the room—at least six feet tall each. The women were pretty, just as I'd seen them before, but I couldn't help remembering how they had looked in my peripheral vision.

They just stared at me in the mirror's reflection, not speaking, or chatting, or moving forward to wash their hands. They had been waiting for me.

I sighed, steadied myself, and turned to face them. "Do I know you?"

"No, but you should," the woman in the center replied.

"I don't recall meeting any of you." My voice wasn't the friendliest.

"You wouldn't," said the one to the right.

I couldn't distinguish them from each other, yet they didn't look exactly alike. It was the oddest thing. I wondered briefly if they were some of Rasputin's lingering followers, but their eyes showed that they weren't vampires.

"You obviously know me. Can you please tell me what you want, so I can get back to my night?"

The one in the center smiled. She wasn't a vampire, but she wasn't human. She didn't move like a human.

"We just thought it was time to make ourselves known," she said.

"Fine. Who are you?"

"We are the Norns," she introduced, holding her hands out to the other women at her sides.

I felt a little shock of electricity in my stomach, but couldn't understand what it was trying to tell me.

"All of you? You don't have individual names?" Maybe I was being slow, but "norns" wasn't ringing any bells.

"You'll learn those in time. Enjoy your evening, we'll be seeing you soon."

They moved towards the exit and their movements flowed into one another as they walked, timed perfectly so that there was almost no space between bodies. *So strange.*

As the last one walked out the door, she turned back to me and said, "Be sure to tell Soren we said hello." She winked, and closed the door.

CHAPTER
FIVE

HER WORDS LEFT ME WITH A KNOT IN THE PIT OF my stomach. *How was Soren involved in this?* Suddenly my overwhelming desire to get home and get naked was far away. I needed answers *now*.

I couldn't bear the thought that he had had something to do with these women and had kept it from me. He knew me well enough to know better than to keep secrets from me—and besides all of that, *who were they, and what the fuck did they want?*

I caught sight of my reflection in the mirror. I looked like a grown-up, and for one of the first times I could recall, I felt *old*. So much for not aging after death. It was in that moment that I realized—age wasn't crow's feet, laugh lines, or dark circles under one's eyes. Age was the accumulation of pain and joy: markings left on your soul that couldn't be erased. It was a cruel irony that some of the most joyous moments of life were also the most painful to reflect upon.

I sighed, and took a moment to admire myself: a vampire, daughter of Loki, a gravedigger, a reaper, a lover. When I died, I was sad that I would never see what I would become when I grew up. I had no idea that death would shape into this. I was so much stronger than I had ever imagined I would be. I didn't want to face whatever was coming for me next. But I knew that I could, and that was good enough.

Soren knew something was up when I came out of the restroom. He knew me, and was good at reading my expression.

I walked up to him, cold and letting him feel the distance I wanted between us. "The Norns say hello."

His face stiffened, but he didn't apologize or defend himself. He didn't try to take my hand or distract me with a kiss. He held the door for me, and we walked quietly. We remained quiet all the way back home.

The mood of the night was done. We walked inside my house, and Soren took off his suit jacket while I kicked off my shoes.

"I'm going to make myself a drink. Do you want one?" he asked.

I nodded.

He set my glass on the table, and for the first time in a long time, we sat across the table from each other instead of side by side on the bed.

I took a small sip from my glass. The drink Soren had made me was good—smooth—but I didn't want a big gulp of it. "How do you know them?" I asked.

Soren finished his drink in one swig, and poured himself another from the bottle he had set on the table. I noticed he was drinking vodka; he was usually a whiskey guy. Normally I would have asked about the change, but not right now. I didn't care what he drank.

"I didn't think it was anything at the time. Rather, I told myself it wasn't anything," he said.

My train of thought shifted; not once had I thought that Soren would cheat on me—until this moment. *Is that what this was about?* I waited for him to go on, and tried to ready myself for whatever was coming next.

"I had taken a soul to the Assignment Hall, and after I had the person in line, I turned to leave and there was a woman standing behind me—right behind me. When I tried to excuse myself and go around her, another woman stepped forward to block me, then another on the other side. I asked if they could move so I could be on my way, and they smiled. I knew they weren't normal women—they were way too tall, and just looked... not right. They parted for me to walk between them, and as I moved, one put a hand on my shoulder. She said, 'Soren, you should tell her she can't win against fate.'" Soren paused, and took another drink of vodka. "I realized later that they must be the Norns."

"Why didn't you tell me this when it happened?" I leaned back and crossed my arms against my chest in a move that wasn't physically comfortable, but made me feel less vulnerable.

"You handled taking care of your fate. I just assumed Loki was trying to scare you or something. There's no cure for vampirism, no way to restore your soul."

I didn't answer, I just sipped my drink.

"They shouldn't be able to touch you. Right?" he asked.

"Who and what are they?" I asked, ignoring his question.

"They are the Norse equivalent of the Greek fates,"

he answered.

I had assumed as much.

"Hel, can they take you from me?" His eyes were almost fearful, a look I had never really seen in Soren.

I shrugged, but felt almost numb about it. "I don't know."

"What are you going to do?"

"I suppose I'll try to find out some more about them, if I can. Maybe I'll ask Persephone and Hades, or Melinoe. But I have the feeling that if this is serious, they'll be back." I finished my drink, and was grateful the alcohol was keeping my emotions in check. I was trying not to worry. I had been assured so many times that once you were a vampire, that was it... but I also didn't know any vampires in my particular situation.

Soren reached his hand out across the table for mine. I uncrossed my arms and placed my hand in his.

"Helena, my love, are you still angry with me for not telling you?" Soren asked.

I shook my head. "No, I understand why you didn't tell me. I'm so tired of fighting against something."

He squeezed my hand. "You have to learn to enjoy the fight. To crave the blood, and the death. Moments of peace are where you rebuild and prepare for the next battle, not where you live."

Wise words from my warrior. I looked into his cold eyes and wondered how much blood and death those eyes had seen, how many lives those strong hands of his had taken.

"I understand the excitement in winning the battles, but what happens when you finally lose?" I asked.

He grinned, "There's always another battle to prepare for."

I sighed and looked down at my pretty gown. "Thank you for all of this: the dinner, dancing, letting me get dressed up. I'm sorry it got messed up."

"Helena." Soren said my name in a deep voice that made me look up at him. "Come here, and kiss me."

For one of the first times I could ever recall since meeting Soren, I wasn't in the mood for sex, but I did want to share a kiss with him, in appreciation of all of the effort he had put into our date. So I stood up and smoothed out my dress, walked over to his side of the table, and leaned down to kiss him.

His lips were warm against mine, and his tongue was hot as it brushed against my own. I started to pull back, but he held me there and kissed me until I felt my muscles begin to relax, and my body begin to take notice.

I sat down in Soren's lap and just kissed him like it was all that I had in the world—and in some ways, it was. We made love to each other through our kiss, and it was almost as good as the real thing. I thought it was, anyway, but after a while Soren pulled back from my mouth nearly panting.

"I need to be inside you," he growled against my neck.

Our fancy clothes soon found themselves on the floor, with no regard to wrinkles or any other cares. The foreplay had been so intense that neither of us cared about dragging it out, we just wanted that final release, so that we could rest, heavy and sleepy in each other's arms.

Afterwards, I didn't want to spoil our relaxed state with "what if's" or pessimistic musings, but I needed him to know what I was feeling. "Soren." I tried to whisper, but my voice came out a little louder than I intended.

"Yes," he answered, and I could tell he was nearly asleep.

"If they can take me away from you…" I started.

"Shh, they'll be no talk of that," he tried to silence me, and pulled me in closer.

"Let me finish. If they take me away from you—from all of you: Boude, Grace, Andreas, Ray—make sure everyone knows how much I love them." I cupped my hand to his face and gently dug my fingers into his skin, not like I was trying to scratch him or get his attention, but like I was trying desperately to hang on. "I need you to know how much I love you, but if I have to leave, find a way to move on."

He was shaking his head in the nearly dark room.

"Please, Soren."

"They're not going to take you." His voice was adamant.

I didn't argue; I hoped he was right. I had a deep sense of unease stirring in my gut that was telling me this was the battle I was going to lose.

CHAPTER

SIX

I KNEW I SHOULD PROBABLY GO INTO THE CITY TO see Persephone and Hades, to get an idea of what I might be dealing with concerning the Norns—I just wasn't up to it. I didn't have good memories of the palace, and my inner strength was wavering.

Soren was already out digging, and I felt envious, because that was all I really wanted to do myself: be outside, digging in the dirt, laughing and working with him and Billy. It didn't take me long to throw on my work boots and grab my shovel and flashlight from the shed.

I settled into a spot with a marker near the two men, and started shoveling. Billy didn't seem to pay much attention, but Soren stopped his own work and watched me.

"I thought you had business to attend to in the city," he said.

I groaned as I accidentally dumped a full shovel of dirt back into the hole I was trying to make, then answered him. "I do, but I wanted to work first."

"Hel," he scolded.

"Leave me alone," I grumbled.

Billy whistled, drawing our attention to him. "Y'all save your bickering. We've got company."

I turned to look behind me, and sure enough, there were two women walking through the brown fields towards us.

One of them had shoulder length black hair, and wore red leather with a matching eye-patch. The other was dressed in something black, with fair skin, tattoos, and black hands.

The two looked absolutely fierce coming towards us. I was glad I knew them, and liked them, and even happier that they liked me.

"Grace!" I called out to my best friend.

She grinned, and broke the serious, badass strut she and Melinoe seemed to have perfected to run to me. She hugged me, and then the two men beside me.

"It's good to see all of you!" she beamed.

"What brings the two of you all the way out here?" I asked.

"Big news!" she gushed.

Melinoe had given us a simple nod that was meant to replace saying "hello," and was standing silently by Grace's side.

Grace grabbed Melinoe's hand and said, "We are going away together!"

I think Grace was expecting more excited reactions from us that matched her own. Instead we all looked at her with puzzled expressions as we tried to figure out exactly what that meant. We were in the underworld, there were only so many places you could go.

Seeing how much Grace wanted me to be happy for her, I put as much enthusiasm into my tone as I could manage. "Oh! That's wonderful! Where exactly are you going?" I tried not sound skeptical or disinterested.

"Mel is taking me on a ship! We're going to sail around the world and underworld!"

I was intrigued, but still very confused. Instead of asking Grace more questions, I looked at Melinoe, hoping she could provide a little more insight.

She seemed happy to explain. "The living world and the underworld are tied together in various places, generally places where ships are known to sink or vanish. If you know what you're doing, you can travel in and out of the worlds and see everything."

"And you do?" I asked.

"I do," she grinned, and pulled Grace in close with her arm draped over her shoulder. Melinoe was definitely sexy, and confidence was not a problem for her, in looks or skill.

"Is there any particular mission, or just a pleasure trip?" I asked, trying not to sound too parental, and probably failing.

"I have to travel frequently," said Melinoe. "I check on the ghosts in different areas, and move along the ones that are ready."

Grace was absolutely beaming. She was so excited about this adventure.

"When are you leaving, and when do you think you'll be back?" *I still sound like a parent.*

"We're leaving as soon as Grace is all packed, and we'll be back whenever we decide the journey is over," Melinoe said in her sexy Australian accent.

Grace sensed my worry. "But you can get in touch with me if you need to! All you have to do is send a message with a ghost, and they can get it to Melinoe."

"That's different," I laughed, envisioning tying a

letter to a ghost's leg like you would a carrier pigeon. Totally ridiculous, I knew, but that's just where my mind went. "OK, that does make me feel better."

"I promise to keep her safe," Melinoe said, and kissed Grace on the cheek.

Grace smiled at Melinoe and stared at her adoringly.

I walked over and hugged both of them. "Look out for each other, and I hope you have a wonderful time."

"I promise to keep in touch," Grace said as she waved and headed back towards the city with Melinoe.

It made me sad to say goodbye to her, but Grace had the spirit of an adventurer, and I knew this was exactly the kind of thing she loved.

Billy and Soren were back to digging, and I picked up my shovel and joined in once more. Soren quirked an eyebrow at me and I rolled my eyes.

"I promise, I'll go into the city after I do this one grave. Let me have my fun," I told him.

"Fine," he sighed.

I started sniffing the air as I dug, trying to get a hint at what might be waiting just below the next foot of dirt. I couldn't smell anything but the dirt itself, like there was no one in the grave. *That's strange.*

I dug a little faster, wondering if maybe they were deeper down, or if it was in fact an empty grave, which would definitely be a bad thing.

Suddenly the smell of rot hit me and I gagged. *What on earth?* I kept digging, trying to breathe through my mouth, and then my shovel touched something.

I cleared the dirt away from the body, and was horrified to see a half-decomposed corpse. That shouldn't have been possible: bodies that had been destroyed or mangled or dissolved in acid usually came through to us looking better than the ones that had suffered less gruesome injuries—something about the way the soul pieced itself back together—and bodies didn't decompose on this side.

The skin was varying shades of brown and green, and I could only guess by the long strands of dried out hair that person had been a woman. There were no clothes on the body that I could see, so that wasn't helpful either.

My mind was having trouble even comprehending that it was, in fact, a person or soul. Right now it was a "thing," and I was not looking forward to waking it up.

I started to call to Soren or Billy to see if they had ever encountered such a thing, but protocol would be the same either way. I might as well get it over with, and ask for help after I raised this person, if I still needed it.

I clicked on my light and shined it in the vicinity of where the eyes should be in the corpse. The body sat straight up, and to my horror, grabbed my arm with a grip so fierce I felt it crack the bones of the corpse's fingers.

I gasped and tried to pull away, too frightened even to scream. A ripple that started at the top of the head ran down, transforming the horror-movie-sight into a beautiful, tall, blonde woman. It was one of the Norns.

She winked at me and then let go as she disappeared before my eyes. I was sitting alone in the grave now trying to process what had just happened. *Did I hallucinate that whole thing?*

I looked down at my wrist where she had held on so tightly, and saw a few fading red marks. *Nope, that just happened.*

"Soren?" I called as I stood up and dusted myself off.

He walked over to me. "You look pale," he said. "What happened?"

"I'm not sure." My head was spinning and my vision was suddenly very blurry. "I think I need to see Boude or Andreas and eat."

Soren looked at Billy, who said, "I'm good here. Take her."

He put my arm around his neck and helped support me as I walked. The farther we walked, the worse I felt, and the less I could see.

"Am I taking you to the boutique or to the Quarter?" Soren asked me.

"Boutique," I gasped. "It's closer."

After I stumbled over my own feet and nearly took both of us down, Soren scooped me up in his arms and I laid my head against his chest.

"Helena, don't go to sleep. You need to stay conscious," he said firmly.

"I don't think I can," I said weakly. I couldn't make my eyes focus, and my eyelids were so heavy. My body was so weak.

I was just surrendering to the blackness when I heard the ding of the bell on the door of the boutique.

"Help her!" Soren shouted as we entered the store, and then the darkness was too much to bear.

CHAPTER
SEVEN

I WOKE TO AN EXTREMELY UNPLEASANT FEELING IN my stomach, and a very bad taste in my mouth.

I sat up and held out my hand. "Going to be sick…" I swallowed hard, trying to delay what was coming as long as I could.

Andreas quickly handed me a small waste basket, and Soren automatically pulled my hair back just before I puked into the can.

It didn't taste or smell like vomit—it was dark and thick, and was very obviously nothing but blood. Confused, I looked at Andreas who wouldn't meet my eyes, and Soren gently rubbed my shoulders.

I realized my eyes could focus now, and I no longer felt weak, but something was still wrong.

"What aren't you telling me?" I asked them.

Soren just continued to rub my back, and Andreas handed me the little compact mirror he always had on hand.

I flipped it open and looked at my appearance. I was pale, as expected since I had felt so badly in the previous hours, but I saw the reason for the pity and alarm in my friend's expressions. My eyes were human. I closed the compact and handed it back to Andreas, then turned to cry on Soren's shoulder.

When my tears turned to sobs that robbed me of my ability to catch my breath, Andreas gave me a drink. The alcohol burned my throat, but quickly settled my crying to a more manageable level.

"Whose blood was that?" I asked, pointing towards the trash can.

"Mine," Soren answered, his arms still wrapped around me.

"We thought any blood might be better than none, and you weren't able to hunt," Andreas chimed in.

I understood the reasoning. I kissed Soren on the cheek. "Thank you. I know that must not have been easy for you."

He shook his head. "I didn't have to think about it for even a second."

I gave him a weak but genuine smile.

"Now what?" I asked to whichever of them wanted to give me an answer.

"Now, you do what they ask of you." Soren's voice was deep and emotionless.

I looked at Andreas, and he shook his head. "I don't even know what I could say."

"Do either of you know where I can find them?" I asked.

"I think they find you," Soren answered as he helped me stand.

I gave Andreas a hug and thanked him for trying to help me. "I promise if there's a way, I'll tell all of you goodbye."

The blonde vampire kissed me on the cheek. "I remember the first day you came into my boutique.

You were so plain and boring. I had no idea the amount of shit you were going to drag me into. You keep things interesting. I'll miss you."

I felt my eyes begin to tear up once more. "Stop that."

"Go," he said, and gave me a push towards the door.

Soren held my hand, and walked as slowly as I wanted to all the way back to the fields. I didn't have any idea what to do next or how to prepare. My thoughts were clouded, and my heart was sad. I stopped trying to think, and just focused on putting one foot in front of the other.

Billy ran up to us before we even made it near the houses. "Hel, are you OK?

I nodded and blinked at him. "Yes and no."

His eyes widened, and he stepped back as if he was almost frightened. "You're not a vampire anymore!"

"No, I'm not. It turns out you really can't run from what's meant to happen."

Billy looked even more frazzled now. "Uh, Hel, there's three women in your house waiting to talk to you. I told them they couldn't go in, but they said you were expecting them. Hope you're not mad at me."

I let out a long breath, "I was expecting them. It's fine, Billy." I walked towards the house.

"Do you want me to come with you?" Soren asked.

"No, I'll be fine."

I went into my house to find the Norns sitting side by side on my bed, staring straight at me as I came inside.

"So there's no way to win this, is there?" I asked.

The one in the center shook her head. "Afraid not."

"Then why did the vampirism work at all?"

"We thought it would be a little more dramatic to turn you back into a human after a time. It's been done so rarely, we thought it would be fun," she said.

"It certainly was dramatic," I agreed. "Which one of you bitches was the corpse?"

The woman to the left gingerly raised her hand. Her voice came out in a rasp as she spoke. She was as lovely as the other two women, but something about that voice coming out of those lips was extra creepy. "Do you know why I looked that way?"

"Because you wanted to scare the fuck out of me?" I asked.

She smiled. "No, because I was carrying your soul. A soul not in use decays just like a body. It wasn't me you were looking at, it was a part of you," she sneered.

"I thought once you became a vampire, your soul simply disappeared—just poof, gone—do not pass go, do not collect two-hundred dollars." I wasn't sure they would get the reference, but didn't care.

"We summoned your soul to us, because you haven't fulfilled your destiny. It's been waiting to be returned to you."

"Fucking Loki," I grumbled.

"Your destiny was set before you were even a thought in your father's mind," the middle one said again.

"Fine, what is my destiny. Directing where souls spend eternity, right? If I'm really bad at it, do I get fired?" *Maybe that's my loophole.*

"You won't be bad at it. It's your calling," said the

one on the right. "Believe it or not, we're not here to ruin you or make you miserable. This is your purpose; we want you to be happy with it. How can we make this a good transition for you?"

I felt my resentment soften. It was nice to at least be asked that. "Do I have to leave Soren? My friends?" I asked.

She nodded somberly, "I'm sorry but they can't come with you. Persephone and Hades are continuing their rule over this area, so you will have your own. The souls you judge will be more specific circumstances, and the area you rule will belong to you completely. We will allow occasional visits, though." She smiled, honestly trying to be accommodating.

I wanted to hate her as much as I did the other two, but couldn't quite manage to do so. "Tell me your names," I insisted.

"I am Verdandi," said the one I liked a tiny bit. She pointed to the one in the center. "This is Skuld, and our sister is Urd. We represent that which is coming into being, what once was, and what shall be."

"When do I have to leave?" I asked, steadying myself to hear that I might not have much time to say goodbye to those that I loved.

"Now," said the one in the center. The three women stood up in unison and moved towards me. It was obvious they were prepared to take me by force.

I held up my hands to stop them. "Wait! Don't grab me. I'll go with you willingly. Just let me say goodbye to Soren and Billy."

They stopped their advancement towards me, and looked a little less menacing when they heard that I would cooperate.

The fancy dress that I had worn on my night out with Soren was laid across the chair near my bed. I had picked it up from the floor, but had never taken the time to get it hung in the closet.

"Can I take any of my things with me? Clothes, books, anything?" I asked.

"Whatever you can carry."

I draped the dress over my arm. I couldn't say why I wanted it—I had never been the dressy girl, but it was the only thing I had that would always remind me of Soren. I grabbed my favorite book from my shelf, *A Picture of Dorian Gray*. Ray had introduced me to it growing up, but more recently, Grace had read it and we'd had a lot of fun discussing the book and all of the quotable lines. I wanted to take something that would remind me of each of my friends, but knew I couldn't take that much.

"I know you said visits would occasionally be permitted, but can I write them or communicate with them in some way?"

"There are ways," the nice one reassured me.

"Can we move this along?" nagged the one that was always in the center.

"I guess I'm ready," I said.

CHAPTER EIGHT

I WALKED TOWARDS BILLY AND SOREN, CHEWING hard on my lip, trying to fight back tears. I hugged my dress and book tightly against my chest.

"Hel, what's going on?" Billy asked.

I was certain the scene looked a little foreboding, with the towering Norns walking with one on each side of me and the third at my back. I think they expected me to run, which was tempting, but would be useless.

I tried to not look as hopeless as I felt. "I have to go," I told him.

"For how long?" he asked. His southern Appalachian accent always added a touch of innocence to everything he said. He was far from simple. Billy was intelligent in both common sense and education, but still I always wanted to protect him from bad things.

"I don't know, maybe permanently, but they said we can still visit." I tried to end on a high note.

Billy grabbed me and squeezed me as he buried his face in my hair and cried.

That was way more than my heart could stand, I bit my lip even harder but it was no use. Hot tears poured down my face, and I told him, "You were the first friendly face I saw when I woke up here," I laughed recalling Soren passing me off to Billy when he didn't like my sobbing upon realizing I was dead. "You had better visit me, and take good care of Margaret. She's good for you."

"I will," he sniffed. "It won't be the same around here without you."

"Nowhere will be the same without you. I love you, Billy. Thank you for always being such a good friend to me."

"I love you too, Hel," he said. Billy stepped away so that I could tell Soren goodbye.

The tears were drying on my face, but seeing Soren all stoic and strong, knowing this was hurting him too—it brought a fresh wave of wetness to my eyes. I bit my lip again, and Soren reached out his hand. He touched my lip and came away with a drop of blood that he licked off of his finger.

"No more tears. You are my strong warrior. You do what you are called to do, and I'll love you all the more for it." He stepped closer and kissed me on the forehead. "This isn't the end. You get settled and let us know when we can see you."

I nodded. "Tell Ray, and Boude and Andreas, and of course Grace. Tell them I'm sorry, and I love them so much, and…"

Soren kissed me, stopping my rambling. "I promise," he said as he pulled away. "Now go, stop delaying the pain. Get it over with."

I started to bite down on my lip again, but thought better of it and just ran my tongue across my lips. I still tasted the faint metallic hint of blood. "I love you."

"And I you."

I turned back to the Norns. "I'm ready." I started walking towards the city, but their hands on my arms stopped me.

"That's not the way to where we are going," said the one that was usually silent.

"Which way?" I asked.

"Down," said the Norn.

I found myself laying in the arms of one of the Norns—thankfully the one that I liked—in an open grave that Billy was about to fill in. I knew that I was dead, but this was still creepy, and more than uncomfortable.

"He doesn't have to bury us, right?" I asked. I couldn't stand the thought of asking my friend to bury me alive, even if it wouldn't kill me. Plus, my claustrophobia was pretty bad after being entombed by Hades for so long.

"No, just wait," she said.

Within moments the dirt beneath us seemed to give way, and we were falling down, deeper and deeper. It wasn't a heart stopping, scary kind of fall: it was gentle and slow. It wasn't falling at all—we were sinking.

I waited for the dirt to fill my nostrils and mouth. I waited for the weight of the dirt on top of us to be heavy and suffocating, but those things didn't happen. We sunk down and down until I began to see the tree roots, and then the new world opened up and we were standing.

We were standing near a massive tree, and the three Norns picked up pails of water that were sitting near the trunk and poured it over the roots.

"This is Yggdrasil. This tree holds all of our own levels of the underworld in its branches and roots. One of them will belong to you. We are the caretakers of this tree, and this is our home. The spring of destiny is just over there." Urd pointed to a small grassy area where I could hear the bubbling of water. "We water this tree with that water, and it nourishes all things." The home of the Norns was much more beautiful than I had expected. There was grass, sunshine, fresh water, and this tree that I inexplicably wanted to wrap myself around and hug.

As I looked up among the branches, I could see little glints of light and sparkles—glimpses of the worlds, perhaps.

"Which is mine?" I asked.

Verdandi pointed down towards a tangle of roots near my feet.

"Down? Again?" I asked. Was there ever an end to the depths of death?

They smiled at me. "Your world shall be called Helheim, and for those who come to you, it will be quite the journey. You will decide who enters your realm to stay, and who does not."

"Do I have to take this journey to get to my own world?" I asked. I was getting a little tired of all these "journeys." I was ready to feel settled and keep my ass planted in one place.

"You have a direct path," said Verdandi. "Come stand here."

I did as I was told, but had to ask, "Is there more falling?" Between going to Hell, and being turned, and then coming here—everything seemed to be a sinking,

45

falling, out of control feeling. Maybe that was a lesson for me, to give up control—but dammit, I didn't want to.

"Helheim will be your world, to make how you see fit. But if you need us for guidance, simply come to the tree and ask. We will be happy to help you," said Skuld.

The three of them watched and smiled as I steadied myself.

"I'm ready," I told them, still clutching the items I had chosen to bring along.

There was no falling this time, no rush of wind, or sign of transition that I could perceive. I was simply in their world one second, and then in my own.

My own world of darkness, emptiness, loneliness, I thought as I tried to look around.

I felt like I was outside, yet I could have been inside. There was simply nothing, the darkness wasn't so heavy that I couldn't see anything, yet there was no source of light, and no shadow. *Is this going to be my eternity? The eternity of the souls that come to me? Am I some version of Hell or purgatory?*

I sighed and sat down, not sure of what to do next.

"Hello, daughter," a voice said.

Loki, my father, walked towards me from a place within the darkness. "I wondered when you would be arriving."

"This is my grand destiny?" I asked. I didn't even have the energy to be angry.

"It is!" he said, and raised his arms. "All of this is yours!"

I nodded. "There's not much to it."

He sighed, "You have to create it, dear girl."

I looked at him. It was still nearly impossible for

me to believe we were related. He had such an eerie charm, and I could never decide if I thought he was endearingly boyish and cunning, or attractive like a beautiful venomous snake.

"How?" I asked.

He covered his eyes with his hand, like I was so exhausting. "Hel, you are a goddess. Think it, desire it, and create."

Truthfully, I did keep forgetting that I was a goddess. Goddesses were stunning, and powerful, and in control of their lives, right? At least that's what I had always believed. Even Persephone had tried to set me straight on that last part. Old belief systems were hard to break, though. But... what did I have to lose?

CHAPTER NINE

I LOOKED AROUND MY EMPTY WORLD AND ASKED myself, *If I could create a world, what would I want it to look like?*

First things first, I needed to be able to see—to have a point of light to focus on—and everything else could come after that. I didn't want a sun or moon just yet, for now...

I closed my eyes and imagined exactly how I wanted them to look: tall, ornate, bright street lamps, with flames glowing cheerily inside. I visualized them here and there, illuminating all that was mine to create. The sound of Loki clapping caused me to open my eyes.

"Well done, daughter!" He placed his hand on my shoulder.

All of the lamps were there, precisely as I imagined them. My world was still empty, but less so now. Even the shadows caused by the flickering flames made me feel less empty and alone. I smiled, feeling proud of myself.

"Now what?" he asked.

"How do I know the boundaries of my world?" I asked him.

"You don't have to worry about that. We look out for one another here. There is already a wall in place. You only need to create a place that you will be content to live, and where those that you choose to let stay with you in their death will be happy," he smoothed his red hair and leaned against one of the street lamps I'd created.

"What kind of afterlife am I supposed to create? Am I where good or bad people go?" I mean I didn't want to create an awesome place for evil people.

"You are where souls come in death. Not the ones meant for Valhalla, just souls of people who are some combination of good and bad."

I knew that most people weren't inherently good or bad, but that most of life was lived in shades of gray, and that good or bad actions generally depended on which side of the fence you were on.

"Create your own space first," Loki suggested. "I think that would be most fitting, then you can go from there. Keep in mind, you are in the far North of the underworld, it's a long journey for those who want to come here, and it's cold."

"OK," I said, and closed my eyes to focus. I had never imagined my dream house, and a castle sounded cold and lonely. My cabin was always my home, and I wanted something that cozy, but bigger. I let my imagination take over, and let my new home roll out before me.

I found myself standing in front of a great hall made of stone and wood. The wooden doors were huge, and warmth rushed out when the doors opened. Long tables covered in delicious smelling food filled the huge, open room, and two grand fireplaces roared, keeping everything toasty.

A door at the far end opened to a hallway, with doors upon doors of rooms for me to explore. Of course, I knew what was behind them—I had created the many rooms—but it would still be cool to see them in person.

One large door opened to a stone swimming pool, also kept warm by a fireplace. That had been one of my favorite selfish creations in this place. I imagined Soren coming to see me, and us spending a lot of time in there—naked.

Then there was my personal bedroom. It was as grand and luxurious as I could make it, with a fireplace on one end. A huge four-post bed, covered in silk and soft furs, sat on one side of the room. There was a large comfy couch for reading, and a whole wall of bookshelves already filled with my favorite books, including the one I had brought from home.

I would have been perfectly happy to have wandered around the hall, taking in all of the pretty things I'd created, but Loki stepped into my room, drawing my attention away again.

"Beautiful work," he said as his eyes took in all of the little details I had designed, such as intricate carvings of animals and people along the beams that ran across the ceiling. "I do think you should focus a bit more on the outside. Souls will be arriving soon, and you don't want them coming to an empty world, or having everyone in here all of the time."

I agreed that wouldn't be good. So I followed him back out to the bleakness. Now that I was out here, I realized the lamps I had first designed didn't really go with the style of the hall I'd created; so in the blink of an eye, I changed them. Now they were pillars made of stone and wood, with amber glass housing the flames. *Much better.*

"I'm going to let you finish your work, but I will come back to check on you," Loki said as he started to walk away.

"I wish you would stay," I told him. My words surprised both of us.

He walked over to me and hugged me. I let him. I didn't know him well, as a friend, father, or even acquaintance. All I really knew were the stories I had read about him, and most of those were not flattering. And even though he had helped me when I rescued Raphael from Hell, it was more for his own benefit than for mine. Right now, though, I didn't care. I just wanted company.

"I promise to be back soon, but first there are other matters I must handle. I haven't given you your present yet. It should do until I can return," he said.

I looked at him suspiciously. "Present?"

"Yes, you need a housewarming gift, and I know how fond you are of Cerberus," Loki grinned at me.

My heart leapt before I even saw the puppy.

It looked as though Loki pulled him out of thin air. The dog was as white as snow, with the exception of his black nose and black tipped ears, the dog's eyes were gold, and seemed to go straight through me.

"His name is Garmr, and he will be the guardian of the gate into Helheim," he said as he placed the puppy in my arms.

The little white ball of cuteness licked my face and wagged his tail. I already knew this wasn't your average dog, and even though I loved the cute little guy already, I had no doubts: he was going to be a beast as he grew older.

"Thank you!" I said cheerfully. I truly was so grateful to have a companion.

"Take care of him now, and he will return the favor when he is grown," said Loki.

I looked up to acknowledge his words, but he was already gone.

Garmr was happily cuddled up in my arms as I surveyed my world once more. What did I want to create here? What would the dead want to do when they got here? Did I want it to be a city like Hades and Persephone's version of the underworld—the underworld that I had become so accustomed to? Maybe I could make it my own version of Heaven. I had told Soren once before that if I could do anything, I would go back to my little cabin in my cemetery and dig graves. Obviously, it would be ridiculous to be a gravedigger here, since there were no dead to bury and no dead beneath the ground to dig up.

So how could I keep the feeling that I had had back when I was just a happy little grave digger? The idea came to me instantly: *gardening*.

I closed my eyes and visualized rich, dark, vital dirt, and on top of that, lush, velvety green grass, and a few rolling hills.

I looked around at everything I'd just created, and then chose a large area to serve as a communal garden. I imagined the ground as already plowed, but I didn't plant the seeds or grow the crops. That was something I wanted to do with my own hands—a task that I imagined souls coming to me would also enjoy. There was just something about having your hands in the dirt, planting seeds, having faith that they will grow into something nourishing for our body or beautiful to our eyes.

I thought I would go ahead and create a few homes for souls coming in, but then I thought maybe they would want to make their own homes. Instead, maybe I should provide the materials: trees to be cut down, tools that are already fashioned. Maybe I should let them have a say.

Almost at that exact moment, I heard a noise. *The sound of feet, perhaps? Talking? Is my first soul here?*

Out from beyond where my eyes could see clearly, there was movement in the shadows—then more, and more.

This wasn't one soul coming to me... It was hundreds.

CHAPTER
TEN

I'D HAVE BEEN LYING IF I SAID THAT I WASN'T frightened. I was used to the souls in the other part of the underworld. These souls, though—I wasn't sure about them.

The long shadows created as they moved forward reminded me of tall evergreens standing at the edges of deep woods. Before I knew it, the exact forest I had been picturing in my mind was in front of me. I would have to be careful about that. It did look lovely, though.

I knew they would be looking for instruction and guidance in this afterlife, and since it was mine, they were undoubtedly going to be looking to me. *How did I end up in this situation?* I asked myself.

An image of Raphael came to mind, the day we met, and that inexplicable flood of feelings that overcame me when I first saw him. *Tricks...* my mind reminded me, and my face flushed with angry heat as I recalled where all of that had led.

I refocused myself, and briefly wondered how Raphael was doing now—if he had found Stephanie.

A woman making her way towards me was quite

close now. Garmr was wagging his tail, and obviously very excited to have someone new to pet him.

When I first looked at the woman, she looked worn, and older than she should have. Beneath her eyes were shadows, dark and sunken; her nightgown was torn and thin, like she had been wearing it for ages. She watched the wiggling pup, and started to reach out her hand, then seemed to think better of it, and put it back by her side.

"It's OK," I told her. "You can pet him." I smiled gently.

She grinned, and stepped forward to pat the dog on his head and give him a scratch behind the ears. Then she looked up at me, asking, "Are you Hel?"

"I am," I told her.

"Is it OK that I'm here? We've all been waiting for such a long time, and today the guardian of the bridge said we were finally permitted to cross," the woman explained.

I wanted to ask who the guardian of the bridge was, but didn't want it to seem like I didn't know what I was doing.

"It's fine that you are here. Did you choose to come here?" I asked. I wanted to know why people would come into *my* underworld when they had so many other choices.

"They told us that yours is the place where we would feel most at home," the woman said.

I smiled. "I hope that you do. Do you have more family with you?"

Her eyes welled up with tears, and she unwrapped a small blanket I hadn't noticed that she was carrying. Inside, there was a baby, obviously premature, and no bigger than my hand. The little one opened its eyes and yawned. The baby girl was pink and warm when I touched her arm.

My knowledge of medicine and history from Ray left no doubt in my mind that they had both died during childbirth.

"Do you want a house?" I asked. "Or would you prefer to live inside the hall?"

She looked around, and then her eyes fell upon the hall, standing large and glowing in the light of the nearby flames. "I could live in there, with you?" Her voice was filled with wonder.

"Sure," I said.

"What about my baby?" she asked.

"Of course you can bring your baby," I laughed.

The woman shook her head. "No, my baby isn't growing. She's not going to have the life—or afterlife— she was meant for in this form. Can you help her soul move forward?"

Oh... this one is over my head. Shit. I tried not to let my ignorance show on my face. "Let me get everyone settled, and I'll see what can be done. For now, go into the hall, eat, drink, warm yourself," I told her.

I watched as she entered the hall, and then turned back to see what seemed like an ocean of people in front of me. I saw no possible way that I could interview each of them and give them exactly what they wanted. I needed help—this was more than I could do. Grief rushed over me, and I found it hard to stand. *How am I going to get through this?* I asked myself.

Closing my eyes, I imagined making myself as loud as possible so that I could project my voice to everyone. When I spoke, my voice boomed and vibrated throughout my being. I said, "I am Hel. I'm very honored that this is where you have chosen to spend your afterlife. I want to make things as comfortable for you as possible, while still giving you a purpose. I need you to split into smaller groups. Decide if you want to build your own living quarters, or if you want me to provide them. Decide how you would like to spend your days, and how you want to contribute to serving Helheim. Once you know who wants the same things, come to me with your requests. Women who are here with their children, you may enter the hall at anytime. Come eat, and warm yourself. We will talk of your needs and desires first."

After my little speech, I waited for any signs of anger or uproar, but none came. The groups started separating little by little, and women carrying babies or holding the hands of toddlers started to emerge from the crowd.

My confidence grew just a smidge; I felt somewhat capable. I just had to keep going.

Having everyone divide into groups had been an excellent idea. Within a relatively short period of time, everyone had a home, a job, or some kind of purpose. Their bellies were full, and there was no unrest that I could sense.

I had invited the women that were on their own, both with and without children, to stay in the hall with me. There was still concern for what to do with the souls of the children. Surely this wasn't their purpose, to spend eternity trapped in the body and mind of one so small. I needed to consult the Norns, but I could do that tomorrow.

Yes, *tomorrow*. The lack of day and night and measurable time was something I had always found difficult in the underworld, so here, I remedied that. It was all an illusion, of course; I could no more plan the true workings of a galaxy and its effects than I could design a human. (Big props to God on those things, if he was around somewhere.) I was happy with my fantasy world, though. Sometimes illusions are all that keep us sane.

With all the souls in their respective places, it was time for me to go to bed. To say that I was tired was putting it mildly. I was exhausted, and missed Soren more than ever. I had learned that not all of the souls that came to me were Vikings, or followed the Norse religion. A lot of people ended up here who had never chosen a religion, but had roots in this ancestry. A few told me they chose this afterlife after working off their time in the underworld where I had just been. That blew my mind and made no logical sense when I tried to think about it. But if time truly didn't exist, then I suppose anything was possible. It just hurt my brain way too much to try to understand.

I said goodnight to everyone and left a few men in charge as guards—after they were approved by Garmr, of course.

Heat rushed towards me when I opened the door to my bedroom, and I remembered the fire I had started in the fireplace. With just a thought, the flames shrank down to a slow steady burn that would keep me warm through the night without suffocating me.

I stripped down to my underwear and laid on the

bed. I wondered how all of my friends were, if they missed me, or were angry with me. I wondered when I would be able to send them a message or see them. I felt sad and tired, but not as emotional as I thought that I should feel. Maybe I had become cold and unfeeling after everything I'd been through, or maybe I was just compartmentalizing so many things that I was numb.

To my surprise, the heaviness of sleep began to pull me in. I let it take me under as I pictured Soren's face on the pillow next to mine.

CHAPTER
ELEVEN

DEEP, DREAMLESS SLEEP HELD ME IN ITS GRASP FOR who knew how long. I woke up with a gasp, nearly having forgotten where I was and what was going on. I was surprisingly cheerful and ready to face the day, ready to get to know some of the souls here, maybe welcome a few more in. I could also go see the Norns to ask about the souls of the babies, and see about sending a message to my friends.

Garmr sensed that I was awake and started whining and wiggling at the foot of the bed. I patted the spot beside me, and the happy little pup jumped towards me with a cute little bark that I could tell would deepen as he grew. Odd as it seemed, I thought he already looked a little bigger than when Loki had given him to me on the previous day.

"I guess we should get our day started," I told the dog as I rubbed his warm belly. The dog sneezed in acknowledgement.

I forced myself to get up and realized that the only clothes I had to wear were the ones I had worn the previous day, or my formal black gown that I had brought. Neither seemed like a good option. *Can I create clothes?* I wondered. I guess it couldn't hurt to try.

Jeans tall, soft black leather boots that lace up the front and over the knee, a white shirt with short, yet elegant, slightly belled sleeves, and a black leather jacket that matched the boots, and still worked with the shirt's wide sleeves. I looked in the mirror that I had also just put on the wall, and was pretty impressed with myself. The outfit didn't really look like something I would ever normally wear—well, except for the jeans. The rest of it, however, did look like my friends. This was most certainly an outfit that Grace, Andreas, and Boude would approve of. I guessed that their classy vampiric sense of style had rubbed off on me more than I realized. I smiled at myself and my choices; I did look good—but oh, how I missed them.

Knock, knock, knock, came booming from my door.

"Yes?" I called as I spent a moment fixing my hair in its usual bun. My clothing choice probably called for me to do something a little nicer with my hair, but I decided it was best to start small.

"I do hate to disturb you, My Queen, but we have an issue," a man's voice that I didn't yet recognize explained.

"I'll be right out," I told him, and then looked at Garmr, who was chewing on one of my old work boots. "Probably some sort of land dispute or something simple," I said out loud to the dog, but mostly to myself.

I imagined a bone I thought the dog would like and handed it to him. He decided the thick, heavy new bone was much tastier than an old boot.

The hall felt good to walk down; I held my head

high and tried to project the grace and authority I had been given as keeper of this underworld. I was in charge, I was a ruler, and for the first time I realized: *I am made for this.*

I don't want to be in charge. I didn't ask to be a ruler. I am so not made for this. Were the very next thoughts that roared in my head as I saw the problem.

People, souls, men, women, children, babies… everywhere—and all of them were waiting for me to tell them what to do.

I tried to hide my shock. I thought I was overwhelmed with the amount of souls the day before. This was at least twice as many. I was going to need help. I thought back to the Assignment Hall and the way that Persephone ran her underworld. The problem was that I didn't know any of the souls well enough just yet to trust anyone to do exactly what I asked in regards to all of these people. It was one thing to ask a few of them to open doors, or clean dishes, or stand guard. It was another to have them help me sort people into their perspective areas, and find ways to give them jobs that would help them contribute to Helheim and keep them feeling useful. I couldn't see that I had a choice though.

Once more I gave my little speech to the crowd about splitting into groups, and separating the women with small children. That seemed like a good starting point again. Then, I called a meeting of the people who had come in the day before. I explained that I needed an area for people to be sorted, a system to get them where they would be happiest, and people to run this. Several men and women jumped at the chance, and I agreed we should give it a try to see if it was going to work.

I created a small but efficient building that resembled my hall, with living quarters in the back for those that would be taking on these rolls. All of the souls would filter through there after coming through the gate. Questions would be asked about why they had chosen Helheim to spend eternity, as well as questions about what occupation they'd held in life, and if they had been happy. Then they decided if they wanted to be a worker, a guard, or something a little less demanding. They got to choose if they wanted to live in one of the homes I made, or if they wanted to build their own. People could garden, or eat in the hall. They could do just about any task they had done when they were alive. The only thing expressly forbidden was harming or harassing one another. I warned people that *that* would get them cast out of Helheim with no possible option of returning, and that if that happened, I didn't know, or care, what would happen to their soul afterwards.

After observing the new assignment system I put into place and feeling satisfied with its efficiency, I decided to go visit the Norns to get the answers to my few lingering questions.

I made my way to the roots of the great tree, where they had told me to come if I had any questions. I wasn't sure how contacting them worked. *Do I just ask my question to the tree and they hear me? Or will I be transported back to where they are? If I don't disappear, or get an immediate response, how do I know if they heard me?*

The roots sprawled out before me, thick and dark.

They rose above me, forming their own sort of tree-like structure, even though there were no branches or leaves—it was all roots, all feeding into the great tree whatever-they-called-it.

"OK," I said aloud, "I have questions. I need some help." Then I remembered my manners and added, "Please."

Nothing happened. I walked to different areas of the roots and touched the offshoots that stood out to me. I repeated myself a few times until my voice was clearly annoyed.

"You said I could call on you for guidance. So where the hell are you three? Or send Loki! I just need some answers!" I bitched, and ended my rant with an angry kick to a root that was about shin height, and heard it crack.

"DO NOT do that," an equally angry voice replied.

I looked up to see the three tall Norns standing in front of me. They didn't look too pleased. That was OK, though—I wasn't happy either.

I crossed my arms. "If you don't want me taking out my frustration on the stupid tree, then you should answer the first time I call."

"Yggdrasil, is not a stupid tree. She is the home for all of us, and you should be grateful," Urd snapped.

"I'm sorry," I said sincerely. "It's just, you ripped me away from the people I loved and expected me to step into the role of this goddess that I don't want—or know how to—be. I need some help."

"I'm sorry we weren't here the exact moment you snapped your fingers and asked for us. You've just done so well that we thought you didn't need us. We were actually quite impressed that you hadn't come to

64

us before now."

I wrinkled my forehead trying to think, "Well I mean, it's really only been a day. Did you think I'd need you in the first hour?"

"My sweet girl," said Skuld, "it has been years."

"What?" I asked in a voice so deep and horrified, I barely recognized it as my own.

"Did you think just because you set time to your own liking in your world that it worked the same everywhere else?"

I felt cold, and sick, and was unable to form words or thoughts beyond, *Oh no...* The truth was, it hadn't even occurred to me. I hadn't been warned of any rules or consequences that I was subject to, I had just been told to create an afterlife as I saw fit. *My God, how long has it been? Have my friends given up on me? Soren.* A knot in my stomach tightened painfully.

I tried to speak a few times before I was able to make a sound. "I—I... uhh..."

"Yes? Out with it."

"I need to get a message to my friends. How do I do that?" I asked. "And how do I know the difference in times between underworlds, so I don't lose time like this again?"

Verdandi answered me, "When you need to send a message to another underworld or afterlife, simply come here and tell Ratatoskr. He will take your message to the appropriate person, or the next messenger who can deliver it.

"Who is Ratatoskr?" I asked.

At that very moment, a large gray squirrel with a fluffy tail scurried down the roots of the tree, stopped at my feet, and looked at me expectantly.

"That is Ratatoskr. He's the best messenger in all of the underworlds," Verdandi smiled, a hint of pride in her voice.

"The squirrel is the messenger?" I asked, making sure I understood all of this correctly.

"Yes, who better to deliver messages between worlds? They are extremely intelligent, and move quickly," she said.

I looked down at the cute little face and wondered if he would really carry a message for me all the way to the fields of the dead. "Can you deliver a message to the reaper, Soren?" I asked.

The squirrel didn't move or respond in any way, it just stared at me with its tiny black eyes.

I looked up at the Norns. "Do I just tell him? What if he can't deliver it for some reason?"

Uld chuckled and the other two grinned. "He'll get it there," said Uld.

"You said before that I could have visitors, or go visit my friends. Is that still right?" I asked.

"We wouldn't suggest leaving your area without having a proper backup in your place," said Skuld.

"But can my friends come here? Just for a visit?"

They looked at each other, and seemed to speak without using words or moving their lips. "Yes, I think it would be OK for them to visit, but you would have to meet them at the bridge or the guardian would never let them cross," said Uld.

I nodded, and looked back at the squirrel. "I need you to please tell Soren to bring everyone, Ray, Grace, Boude, Andreas, Billy, whoever they want to bring— bring them here to visit, and I'll meet them at the bridge."

Ratatoskr looked at the Norns and then back at me, then back at them.

"Why isn't he leaving?" I asked.

The fuzzy little messenger started making a strange chirping sound that was unquestionably angry.

"Very well!" sighed Skuld. "He says it will take much too long for them to make the traditional journey. He says he'll deliver the message, but in order to keep our agreement to you, we need to meet your guests and bring them through the shortcut," she said, as she rolled her eyes.

The squirrel calmed down.

I winked at him and said, "Thank you for looking out for me." And I swear I think he winked back.

CHAPTER TWELVE

BECAUSE THE NORNS HAD TRIED TO TRICK ME, I wasn't sure how I felt about asking them anything else. I still needed to know what to do with the souls of the children that needed a different place to move on to. I wondered who I could ask. Now that I had Ratatoskr to send messages to my friends, my circle wasn't as narrow. When he returned from this task, I could send him to ask Persephone; she would know what to do.

The Norns had promised to bring my friends to visit me, and I anxiously awaited their arrival. In the meantime, I could see how everything was running back in my world.

I was happy to see that things were running pretty smoothly. The assignment system I put in place was efficient. As I walked around, I saw people tending to the garden, building their homes, and engaging in imaginary battles with dull swords they had fashioned.

The men and women saw me watching, and were suddenly nervous. One of the women approached me.

"My Queen, is it alright that we are still practicing

for battle? We mean no harm, it's just what we do," asked the strawberry blonde. She was covered in dirt and out of breath, but she was smiling.

"Of course!" I told her. "Is there anything else you need that might make your battles, or your time here, better?"

"If we could have stables with horses!" Her eyes lit up as she made her suggestion.

"I'm not sure about creating animals, but I'll see what I can do," I told her.

"Oh, thank you!" she exclaimed, and rejoined her friends to share the news.

This was good. I was making a difference. This feeling was better than the terror I was fighting back waiting to see if the squirrel could find my friends. I couldn't help my mind from rushing back to that moment—"*years*", she had said.

What if Soren is gone, or thinks that I have forgotten him? What if Grace or the other vampires are dead or don't want to see me? I wished that someone had told me about the dangers of creating time.

I went towards the hall, and the two guards I had assigned opened the large doors for me. The wooden doors creaked on their large metal hinges, and I recalled the sound of the old gate in my cemetery. Even when life changes, little things remain the same.

Laughter and voices boomed inside the hall. Men, some with long beards cackled like little children, throwing their heads back and wiping amused tears from their eyes. Women stood in corners, whispering and discreetly pointing. Little children ran around the room chasing one another in games of tag and such. As afraid as I was for my life (or whatever this was) to be completely different once again, I knew that it wouldn't be all bad.

Upon realizing just how well I was dealing with this pain and uncertainty, I had to wonder if I was growing too cold, too used to awfulness and heartache. But my heart didn't feel totally broken this time—at least not yet.

I picked up a metal cup from one of the long tables and sipped the liquid inside. It was delicious red wine, only the metal of the cup had mingled with the flavor. No one had complained yet, but I couldn't imagine too many people would enjoy the aftertaste. To me, it tasted like blood, and took me back to my days of being a vampire. I smiled, recalling my hunting trips with my friends. *Hmm, I wonder if I could make my own version of vampires,* I considered.

I went into the back of the hall where the living areas were, and one of the women who was staying ijn the hall sighed and came towards me carrying a much larger puppy than the one I had left.

"You have to take him with you next time you leave the hall," she said sounding quite exasperated. "He's done nothing but whine at your door and growl at everyone who has walked by."

I laughed and took the dog in my arms, handing the woman my cup of wine. "My goodness. You are getting so big, so fast," I told the now happy pup, and kissed him on the head.

The woman laughed. "Hellhounds do that," she said, and walked off before I could ask her name again. I was trying to learn names, but there were just so many people.

"Are you a hellhound?" I asked Garmr, with a bit

of surprise in my voice. I knew that's what Cerberus was, and it made sense; but still, that was not a breed of dog you ever plan to own.

I put him down on the floor and clicked my tongue for him to follow me. We walked the halls for a while, just checking things out, and wandered towards the back of the long building.

I stepped into the area with the large pool, and the warmth and blue waters called to me. "Want to go for a swim?" I asked the dog.

Garmr backed away from the pool and appeared to almost shake his head. "I guess hellhounds don't like to swim," I said, and then looked around the room to be certain no one else was in there.

Bathing suits weren't a thing I had given much thought, but I was alone and didn't care right now. I just wanted to feel the water on my skin, and to swim. I couldn't remember the last time I had been swimming. It had been sometime before I had died; I hoped it was like riding a bike.

I took off my clothes and made sure my hair was up out of my face, and then I slowly walked into the pool, shallow end first. Yes, I could have just jumped, but I wanted it to be a slow, easy transition.

The water was as warm as bathwater, and it felt amazing as I descended into it, feeling it rise around my body. I floated for a while, staring up at the tall ceilings and intricate beamwork. Then I swam a few laps, and realized it was still possible to be dead, and a goddess, and feel out of shape. So I floated some more.

I was luxuriating, totally relaxed, letting the water hold my body so gently and delicately. Floating requires surrender, and control at the same time. I had

71

always enjoyed floating when I was alive, but could never maintain it for long without moving a little too much and falling beneath the surface. Now, I could do it forever.

It was while I was calm, and peacefully lying in (or maybe *on*) the water, that a gentle wave lapped around me. The water should have been still with just me in it. I opened my eyes to see a man standing over me. In total shock, I went under the water, gasping as I did so. Big mistake.

Sharp pain filled my nose and throat; it stung and burned to inhale water into all of those delicate places that water isn't supposed to go.

I thrashed and tried to gain my footing, but I was in the deep end. I knew that I needed to swim, but couldn't get past all of the water wanting to pour down my throat and into my lungs, while the water I had already imbibed was trying to come back out.

Two large hands grabbed hold of me and lifted my head and chest up out of the water. The man's grip was tight, and I was disoriented, drifting in and out of consciousness.

I felt pressure on my abdomen, and lips against mine, just before a rush of hot water poured out of my mouth as I coughed.

So naturally, the first thing I said after I recovered was, "Did you try to drown me, or kiss me?

"I was trying to save you!" The man's voice was deep, but he sounded amused.

"Are you sure you didn't try to drown me?" I asked,

as my vision started to clear and my throat didn't feel quite as much like I had swallowed lava... maybe just a pot of boiling water.

"Quite sure. You seemed to be doing a fine job trying to drown yourself, though. I apologize if my introduction startled you into such a fit," said the man.

My rescuer was beautiful: his skin was almost golden, and his eyes were the brilliant color of a turquoise sea. His brown hair was sunkissed, and fell just above his broad shoulders. He didn't have a full beard, just a little scruff, and he was broad-shouldered with a narrow waist.

The man looked nothing like Soren, yet had the same kind of strength in his demeanor, only with more humor in his eyes.

"You don't just stand over someone who thinks that they are in a pool by themselves, and peacefully lost in their own little world," I said, slightly annoyed at the implication that I was such a mess.

"Well, it is a pool for all, right?" he asked.

"Yes, but there was no one in here when I got in."

"Right, but I wanted to swim, and you were naked. I thought it was the polite thing to do to let you know I was also swimming in here, in case you wanted to leave or wear something," he looked down at my breasts as I sat up, and gave me another amused smile. "I mean, you were perfectly welcome to stay and join me, since I don't mind being naked either. I just thought it was the polite thing to do." He looked down at his own nude body, and my eyes wandered over him as well. *Fair is fair.*

"Who are you?" I finally asked the handsome stranger.

The man rose up on his knees, and gave a graceful bow, reminding me of Boude. "I am Baldur, My Queen."

I was taken aback at the answer, although I supposed that I really shouldn't have been. I remembered that Baldur was a god himself, and recalled the stories that I had read about his mother, Frigg, trying to protect him. She had asked for a vow of protection from all the many flora and fauna of earth, and had only forgotten one small plant-- the mistletoe--because she thought it was too small to be harmful. Then I recalled the rest of the story.

I clasped my hand to my mouth. "It was Loki, my father, who killed you," I said in horror.

Baldur laughed a loud and booming laugh. "Indeed it was, the stories are true." He shrugged. "But it's what we do with one another—the gods I mean. If they hear someone is invincible, they just can't help but keep poking in search of a weak spot."

"You don't mind that he killed you?" I asked.

Baldur shook his head. "When it's your time, it's your time, no matter who shoots the arrow."

That's an interesting way to look at it, I thought.

"Are you feeling alright after your incident?" he asked.

I inhaled and was happy to realize it didn't burn and sting like it had before. "Yes, I think I've recovered."

"Excellent!" Baldur cheered. "Let's get dressed and meet in the dining hall—a place where we can talk more—shall we?" His smile was beautiful, and he made me feel warm in ways that I hadn't in a very long time.

He stood up first and offered me his hand. I took it, and

he quickly pulled me up onto my feet. My body swayed forward and I fell into him, naked body to naked body. Our heights were just right so that a very delicate part of him was right against a very delicate part of me, and I gasped. I felt my face pale with the shock of it all, as all the blood in my body rushed to my feet.

I stepped back and closed my eyes, trying to ground myself. *No no no… Think of Soren.* I reminded myself.

"Sorry," I said.

"As am I," he said. "Even though I'd be delighted to take things further, if that is your wish."

He was looking me straight in the eyes. My body was awake now, desire rushing through me like it hadn't in some time—like I hadn't been with anyone in years. *But that's crazy, I just left Soren only a few days ago. Only by my time, though—by his it has been years. Am I feeling both?*

Baldur waited for me to respond, and I tried to think of what to say, but I still didn't feel steady on my feet. I put my hand to my head and closed my eyes, trying to gain some kind of clarity.

"Perhaps, we should save this conversation for another time. Let me take you to your room to rest," he offered.

I nodded in agreement, and said, "First, we should probably get dressed."

"Wise decision, My Queen," he smirked.

I turned my back to him while I put my clothes back on. Yes, I had already seen him naked, and he had seen me, but I didn't need to add more fuel to my desire.

Once we were dressed, he helped me to my room; I was surprised by how unsteady I was feeling. I'd been hurt plenty of times since I died, but I hadn't nearly drowned before—maybe it was worse.

He opened my bedroom door for me, and I could tell he was waiting to be invited inside; it was the first hint of awkwardness I had witnessed in his demeanor.

"I'm sorry," I said. "You are very handsome, and I appreciate the rescue—even though you kind of caused the accident in the first place," I smiled. "But I don't think it would look good for the Queen to be taking men into her bedroom so soon after her arrival."

"You're more than a queen, you know. You're a Goddess, and more than that, you seem to be a kind one—the most rare of all. Your happiness comes first in the eyes of all of the souls you're looking after, and in mine as well," Baldur smiled.

He was shiny and beautiful, and unlike anyone that I had ever had—but I couldn't think of him in that way until I knew where my Soren was, and if he still loved me. Dammit, why was I always waiting on another man, instead of enjoying the one in front of me? I thought about telling Baldur about Soren, and how I was waiting to see if he came to me, but I didn't need to overshare. I was afraid that it would sound like I didn't want Soren to come back, or like I would be settling for Baldur if he didn't. Neither scenario was true, so it was best to stay quiet.

"Happiness is fleeting," I said, and tried to smile at him, but my voice was tinged with sadness that I couldn't manage to hide.

Baldur reached out to brush the side of my face with his fingertips. It was a gentle comforting gesture.

"Indeed," he said. "That's why one must always be in search of it."

He walked away, and I watched his glorious body

glide down the hall as if he was the king. If nothing else, I hoped that he and I could at least be good friends.

Remembering my puppy that I thought I had left in the pool room, I called out, "Garmr!"

I was answered with a bark that came from inside my bedroom. I opened the door a little wider to see him on my bed, happily wagging his tail, and nearly double the size he had been only a few hours ago.

Relieved, but puzzled, I went over to the bed and scratched him behind the ears until he rolled over, wanting belly rubs. The woman had told me that hellhounds grew fast, and I wondered if that was why he was getting so big, or if it had something to do with the way I had structured time here. I did wish someone had warned me of the dangers of that.

CHAPTER THIRTEEN

IT WAS NEARING EVENING, AND THERE WERE THINGS I needed to do. I needed to go into the dining hall and eat with my people, listen to their concerns, think about ways to make life better here, help the children. Unfortunately, I didn't want to do anything except hide away in my room and alternate between thinking of Soren, and trying *not* to think of Baldur.

I changed my clothes into something more dinner appropriate: A simple but lovely red dress with gold details. Looking at my reflection once again, it wasn't lost on me that my new choices in clothing reflected the styles of my friends that I missed. I touched the soft, silky fabric and remembered my adventures with Andreas and Boude.

The dining hall was booming with loud voices and laughter. Plates were piled high with colorful roasted vegetables, fresh baked breads, and delicious-smelling smoked meats. The fires were kept at a low level so that we weren't living in a sauna, and my guards were keeping a close watch on anyone they thought might get out of hand.

As I stood in the entrance to the hall, just observing,

one of the guards came up to me and asked, "Queen Hel, may I escort you to your seat?"

The man was older, but by no means old. His beard was thick and streaked with gray, and his eyes were blue and wise. He was still strong, but he had lost the drive to fight all the time, like the rest of these men seemed to have.

"You may," I told him.

He took my arm in his and led me through the rows of tables. Truthfully, I wasn't sure where he was going seat me. I hadn't chosen a particular spot for my daily meals. As we neared the other side of the dining hall, I was shocked to see us approaching a beautifully carved throne.

I stopped in front of it and reached out to gently touch the dark wood.

The guard smiled at me. "Do you like it?"

"It's stunning," I told him, then asked. "Who made it?"

"We've all worked on it, anyone who could build or carve. It's been out in one of the sheds, and people have stopped by all day to help," he told me.

Tears stung my eyes as I moved closer. The throne was as tall as me; it was smooth, and polished, and everywhere that I looked on the side or back there was some intricate carving of an animal or flower. The front of the throne was smooth and untouched, and I couldn't resist running my fingers across it.

"That part is unfinished, so we can add details as you rule," he said.

"I don't know what to say," I told him, smiling so that he knew I was happy. "It's absolutely incredible. Thank you."

The man blushed, and seemed pleased that I appreciated their effort. "I hope you enjoy it."

I watched as he walked away back to his regular post, then I looked back at the chair in front of me. *Throne—I have a fucking* **throne**. I couldn't even figure out how all of this was possible.

"Well are you going to try it out?" a deep voice asked me.

I recognized the voice instantly, and glanced over to see Baldur smiling at me, with his hand outstretched to help me step up to the throne and take my seat.

"I don't feel like I deserve it, yet. I'm no one's queen, even if that's what they call me."

Baldur's smile faded and a more serious look took over his face. "You don't have to feel like a queen to be one—in fact, those types usually make lousy queens. Instead, you simply treat everyone like you would want to be treated, and take their wants and needs into consideration. That is why you are a wonderful queen to serve."

I placed my hand in his, and the warmth caught me off guard. I let my fingers linger in his hand longer than necessary as I stepped up to the chair and took my seat. I felt a surge of strength and solidness run through me.

"That smile on your face tells me that you're feeling more at home here than you thought you would," Baldur grinned.

I ran my hands over the smooth wood and looked out at the people in the hall. Everyone was laughing and talking and eating and drinking. I had created this place for souls to find rest, and they were happy here. Maybe I wasn't totally awful at this.

"Enjoy, Queen Hel," Baldur said and started to walk away.

"Baldur." I said his name and he turned around. He was so handsome, and golden like the sun. "Would you sit with me for dinner?"

He motioned to my throne. "I don't think there's room for two in there, unless you are wanting to get very cozy," he teased.

"I meant that I would eat with everyone else, of course. I just haven't really made any friends here yet—and I like you," I told him honestly, and with less hesitancy in my voice than I imagined would be there.

"It would be my honor." He bowed and took my hand once again, this time to help me down.

I sat with him at an empty end of a long table, and began to fill my plate with meat, veggies, and bread. Baldur sat beside me and did the same.

"I would be happy to prepare your plate, if you'd like. The Queen really shouldn't be getting her own food," he said.

Placing another spoonful of apples on my plate, I said, "I'm perfectly capable of making my own plate. However, I would allow you to pour a glass of mead for me." I slid my cup towards him.

Laughing, he filled my goblet and his own from the pitcher of mead on the table. "Anything you wish." He winked a turquoise eye at me.

I took a bite of bread and tried not to let my thoughts about him linger anywhere they shouldn't be.

He settled in beside me. "Tell me about where you came from, about your life before you became the Queen of Hel."

"That's quite a long story," I said.

"We have all the time in the world," he reassured me.

The mead was strong, and the dining hall was warm—as warm as his smile and his intense gaze focused all on me, waiting for me to tell him all about myself. So I did.

I told him about growing up as a gravedigger, I told him about Ray, and Raphael, and the day I died. I told him about being a reaper, and Soren, and hell, and vampires, and everything that I had endured to avoid this fate, and how I had still ended up here.

He listened without reaction. There were no moments of surprise or pity on his face, just intent interest until I finished talking. "How do you feel about all of it now?"

"The past, or being here?" I asked.

"Everything," he answered.

"I miss my friends, and if I could return to them, I would in a moment. But I don't think there's any reason to think like that. It doesn't really matter, does it? I can't shape what happens to me, I can only try to make the best of it." I looked into his eyes and thought very hard about kissing him.

His body shifted, and he started to lean in to meet my lips, before he suddenly pulled back and took a drink of his mead. "This is true," he said. "You are very wise."

I was both disappointed and relieved that he hadn't kissed me. I sighed, and picked up the glass of water I had been ignoring. "Tell me about you."

Baldur's eyes twinkled and his skin looked even more sun kissed in the glow of the firelight. "You don't want to hear about all of my battle conquests," he laughed.

"I might not enjoy every bloody detail, but from the way you lit up when I mentioned it, you have a lot of reasons to be proud, I can tell." I placed my hand on his and felt my body try to move in closer. *Not a good idea.* I moved my hand and purposefully slid away a few inches.

"I am proud of my accomplishments. That might sound barbaric to you, but in my killing others, I kept my own people safe, and that was my only goal."

I searched his face for traces of remorse or regret, just in case those emotions were lurking underneath the surface, but I saw none. "I understand that. There's nothing I wouldn't do for those that I love," I told him.

Baldur held up his cup and I met his with my own. "To those we love," he said.

"To those we love."

CHAPTER FOURTEEN

NIGHT HAD COME ONCE AGAIN, AND IT DIDN'T hold the comfort that I had longed for. I knew that the moments ticking by in my corner of the underworld meant that weeks, maybe even months, were passing by in other places.

Maybe it's time to just let the past go, I told myself. Of course I missed my friends, but missing them didn't mean shit. I wondered briefly if I could go to them—find some way of leaving this place, and visit them just for a short time. Although my intuition told me that if I did that, then I would have a very hard time making myself come back here.

I thought of Baldur's face and how much I had wanted to kiss him. How long was I planning to wait for Soren before I moved on? Maybe he had already, and I couldn't blame him one bit.

Baldur had tried to walk me to my room again this evening, and I stopped him at the door at the end of the hall, before we came to the bedrooms and the rest of the living quarters.

"This is far enough," I told him. "Thank you for keeping me company and having dinner with me."

"It's been my pleasure. Would you be so kind as to join me for dinner tomorrow evening?" he asked in return.

I smiled, "Same place, same time?"

"Yes," he said.

"See you then. Goodnight, Baldur."

"Goodnight, Queen Hel."

I replayed the evening on a loop: him convincing me to get into my throne, talking with him all evening at dinner, and that kiss we came so close to sharing. My body twinged with desire, and seemed to be saying, *Hey, he's hot, we're lonely. Why aren't you on top of him?* Replying with, *Because... Soren,* didn't seem to convince it otherwise.

The bed suddenly gave under the weight of Garmr jumping into it with me. He was definitely no longer a puppy in anyone's eyes. He was nearly the size of Cerberus now, and took up more of the bed than I did.

The big baby laid down beside me and stretched a massive paw across my stomach. I made sure I could still breathe, and then rolled over so that I could snuggle him. It wasn't Baldur, or Soren, but it was still pretty cozy nonetheless. Sleep pulled me in quickly.

A warm wet sensation on my face woke me up. The cuddly doggy-giant that I had fallen asleep beside was now licking my face.

I opened my eyes, expecting to see light coming through the window, telling me that it was time to get up and figure out what to do and where I was needed for the day. To my surprise, it was still dark in my room, except for the small fire gently burning in the fireplace. I tried to push Garmr away and roll over to fall back asleep, but a deep and disturbing growl trickled from the dog's mouth, and a sense of unease slowly crept up my body.

Garmr was still in the bed beside me, and while the growl wasn't getting worse, and he wasn't making a move to attack whatever was in the room, there was most certainly something or someone in here with me.

There were things in my room that I could use as a weapon, but I didn't know where my attacker was. The last thing I wanted to do was roll over and see a face staring at me, but I needed to face who or whatever was coming for me.

I slowly slid towards the head of the bed and sat up with my back against the headboard. I placed a hand on Garmr's back, for my own reassurance and his. Then, I let my eyes scan the room, searching for the source of the distress. I saw nothing.

For a brief moment I thought of asking, "Who goes there?" But that would just be way too silly. I felt myself smiling at my kookiness, even though I was simultaneously terrified. My past had really warped some aspects of how I processed fear.

"Who is there?" I asked, but received no answer. "The dog and I know you are in here. Show yourself now!" I ordered. I steadied my nerves and made the smoldering fireplace flare to life, expecting to see the worst in front of me.

I was ready to fight if need be, but I couldn't fight someone I couldn't see, and I couldn't see whatever was in this room.

Garmr was still growling, and his focus was on

something near the wall just by the door. From my position in the bed, I couldn't see anything out of place. I got up and walked over there, and just when I was about to scold Garmr for scaring me out of my mind, I saw movement.

It was a hard thing to explain, since it looked as though nothing was there. How does nothing move? But—it did.

I brightened the light in the room once more with lamps on the wall, and then I finally saw him. Translucent and damn near invisible, a ghost was standing quietly and mindlessly by my door.

"Shit!" I screamed and jumped back, I was closer to him than I initially realized. He blinked at me.

"Did I frighten you?" he asked in a barely audible whisper.

"Uh, yeah. Yeah, you did," I told him as I regained my composure. "Who are you and what do you want?" I asked him, and in almost the same instant I realized there was only one person I knew who would send a ghost: *Melinoe.*

Before he could even answer, I cut in with, "Did Melinoe and Grace send you?"

The ghost nodded. "Yes, my mistress has had me searching for you for a long time. The furry one brought us a message," he said.

"What about Grace? Is Grace still with your mistress?"

"She is," he said.

"Where are they? Can you take me to them or bring them here?" I wanted to grab the front of his shirt and shake him so that he would answer faster.

"They cannot get through the wall, which is made

only for the dead that belong here. But if you can leave, I will take you to them. They are waiting at the river," he said simply.

Fucking walls. I recalled the one in the other part of the Underworld, and how it connected all the other afterlives. *Well, obviously not all of them.*

"OK, let me get some things together, and I need to let someone know that I'm leaving. You stay here, and we'll leave as soon as I'm ready," I ordered.

"I understand," whispered the ghost.

CHAPTER
FIFTEEN

I WANTED TO PUT MY BOOTS ON, GRAB THE DOG, and be on my way, but I had no idea how far I would have to go, or how long I would need to be gone. I didn't know if I needed to leave someone in charge, or if whoever I told would try to stop me from leaving. I wasn't even entirely sure how to leave this world; none of that mattered, though. My friends were waiting for me—I would figure it out.

In my tizzy of throwing clothes onto the bed, I knocked over the heavy, iron candelabra that was near the door. The object fell against the stone floor with crash that sounded considerably louder than I wanted it too. *Dammit.* I was trying not to draw attention to my departure.

I held my breath for a moment, waiting to see if anyone was going to come through the door and check on me. I was half annoyed, half relieved when they didn't.

"Could you turn around please?" I asked the silent and nearly invisible ghost, who I had nearly forgotten about until I started to disrobe. I saw a faint movement against the wall and assumed he had done as I'd asked.

My sleeping gown was on the floor and my pants were halfway up my legs when my bedroom door flew open and someone burst in.

I spun awkwardly and nearly fell, since my pants weren't all the way on.

Baldur's hair was tangled and wild, and his eyes were still half filled with sleep. He was holding a sword and was half naked.

"What the hell are you doing?" I yelled as I finished pulling up my pants and then tried to cover my breasts with my arms.

"I heard a crash, I came to check on you," he murmured, and straightened his back as he tried to appear more heroic.

"That was several minutes ago—I would have already been dead... or something. Where were you when you heard it, anyway?" I asked.

"I took a room two doors down from yours so I could keep an eye on your safety. I wanted to be next door, but they wouldn't trade with me."

"First of all, it's a little creepy you didn't tell me you were staying so close... And second, would you please turn around so I can dress?" I motioned my hand for him to turn around.

"It's nothing I haven't seen before, and I'm topless as well," he winked.

"Just the same."

He turned around and I quickly finished dressing.

"So why are you knocking things over and getting dressed in the middle of the night?" Baldur asked.

I took a moment to think about whether or not I should tell him, but I needed to tell someone, and I felt like I could trust him.

"My friends are here—well, they're at the river unable to get through the wall. I need to go to them and bring them here. I have to see them," I said, and could hear the desperation in my voice.

"Go, I'll look after things for you," he urged.

"Really? I can trust you to keep things in order?"

"Of course you can. I'll also walk you to the gate. I promise things will be just as you left them when you return."

I finished tying the lacing down the front of my blouse, and went to him. I kissed him lightly on the cheek. "Thank you."

"Of course, My Queen," he replied, his eyes locked with mine and held all of the words he resisted saying.

I felt the hair at the back of my neck prickle, and almost wished that I had time to linger in the moment of tension between us.

We sneaked out through the hallways and past the few guards that I had stationed around the great hall. The one who saw us simply smiled at us, as if he thought that Baldur and I were on a romantic midnight stroll. Melinoe's ghost didn't attract any attention, and Garmr seemed the most excited of us all, happily running along wagging his long tail. His body was hip height to Baldur now—big puppy.

Outside, the air was chilly, and the moon was just a sliver of gold up in the sky. We all walked closely to one another as we passed by the small farms and houses where everyone was resting.

"How far are we from the wall?" I asked.

"Not too far. Maybe a mile," Baldur answered.

I turned in the direction of the ghost, "How far is the river from there?"

"From this side, it's not too far. The journey to the river was very long," the ghost replied.

It was a little unnerving to be speaking with a person I couldn't see, but I had become used to things like that.

We were silent as we walked, and if Baldur got too far ahead, I'd quicken my pace to catch up once more. I was desperate to get there quickly, but my mind was so busy I couldn't force myself to keep a quick pace.

The silhouette of the wall came into view, and torches illuminated the perimeter. It wasn't a smooth wall, like the one back in my old underworld; things were poking out from the sides, and the top edge was uneven and rough. I stared at it, trying to figure out what the wall was made up of.

Vines twisted up and around stones of gray and bone-white. I walked closer to look at the stones and things that jutted out of the wall. I leaned in closely to examine the odd shape of a particular stone, and jumped back with a gasp when I saw the empty sockets of where eyes had once stared out of the worn skull.

"Bones—bodies," I whispered. "The wall is made of bodies."

Baldur's hand patted me on the shoulder and I jumped again, even though it was meant to reassure me. "It's a wall of the dead. It's meant to inspire fear for those not meant to be here."

I stared at it again, and ran my fingers across a small bone that ran horizontally in between a few rocks and other bits and pieces.

"Does it really bother you—Queen of the Dead?" he asked.

I cocked my head to the side before I answered, "I suppose not. I just wasn't expecting it."

I hated to admit that I kind of liked the extra protection this wall offered around my little world. I wasn't sure who we were keeping out, but I was probably OK with making them stay there.

"Are you ready to cross?" Baldur asked me.

"I know the gate is guarded, but am I supposed to climb the wall?" I asked. *Not the first time that I'd used bones as a ladder.*

"You're the creator of this world. Make your own way through," Baldur suggested.

I closed my eyes and imagined all of the vines that wound around the bones shrinking back and pulling apart enough to make an opening for us to go through. When I opened them, there it was.

"Thank you," I told Baldur. "I wish you could come with us."

"I wish that I could as well, but I've already promised you that I would look after things here. Just remember: you are more powerful than you give yourself credit for," he smiled and touched my shoulder.

I stepped through the magical door first, followed by the ghost, and then of course Garmr wanted to make his way through as well, when I saw Baldur shaking his head.

"I wouldn't let him accompany you. The giants sometimes like to make a snack of dogs," he warned.

"Whoah, wait a minute, giants? No one said anything about giants," I said, and almost came back through the doorway.

"You'll be fine. You probably won't even see any. Keeping Garmr here is just a precaution."

The dog was looking back and forth between us like he was waiting for a final decision.

I couldn't even fathom anything that would make a snack out of a hellhound. "You're staying," I said to the dog, who sighed in disappointment. I patted him on the head. "I appreciate your loyalty, but I need to keep you safe." I kissed his soft white head, and he sulked off to Baldur.

"Safe travels. We anxiously await your return," Baldur said, and dipped his head to me.

CHAPTER SIXTEEN

LEAVING MY CORNER OF THE UNDERWORLD MEANT that I didn't know what I was stepping into next. I followed the nearly invisible ghost, and made one or two sad attempts at conversation. I knew they didn't really like to talk that much. Ghosts were ghosts because they were still so hung up on their mortal lives, and they preferred to be back in the land of the living; they were only in the underworld when Melinoe called them here for a job.

We walked and walked. To me, it felt like walking through a dark hallway, only less claustrophobic. It wasn't truly dark, and we didn't need a light, but it wasn't sunny or well lit either. It was just...empty, for a long way.

The longer we walked the more nervous I became. I honestly didn't know if Grace would be happy to see me, or what I was walking into. Sure, for me it had only been days, but they had been long days to me, and as much as I hated to admit it, my own memories of the world before this were fuzzier than they should have been. "Years..." the Norn's voice echoed once more in my head.

In the distance, I made out the shape of a man walking towards us—the first other person we had encountered. He was nearly dragging his left leg, and he looked old and tired. As he approached, I could hear him mumbling something. I listened harder and realized he was saying, "Hel," over and over again.

Once he was close enough, I said, "Hello."

He stopped walking and mumbling and stared at me. He looked me up and down with a strange look in his eye, and I almost stepped back, recalling the time I was mauled by a crazed vampire.

"Hel," he said again softly.

I wasn't sure if he was calling me Hel, or asking if I was her, or if he was asking where it was. I pointed the direction we just came from and said, "It's not much farther, that way."

He stared at me for a moment longer, and then shuffled off. I wondered if I would recognize him once I got back.

We continued walking, and everything seemed to be getting lighter. I wondered if there was "day" and "night" in the rest of the underworlds here, or how far my own creations stretched. I was able to see the path we walked along was dirt, and beyond that, there really wasn't much to see.

"How much farther?" I asked the ghost.

He stopped and said, "Not much longer."

We trudged on and I began to hear a noise out in the distance. At first I thought it was thunder, but it sounded too sharp to be thunder. It almost sounded like metal, and the closer we walked, the louder it got. It sounded like the screams of dying men, and clanging of swords and axes. It sounded like a battle.

"What's going on?" I asked, ready to turn back, or run towards the sound to save my friends if they were in danger.

"That is the river. It mimics the sounds of war and death," he said.

"Oh." *That doesn't make me uncomfortable at all.*

I saw a bridge as we approached, and walked towards it.

"No, the giant lives on the bridge; she would never have let us cross. They sailed under it. The boat is hidden just out of sight," the ghost told me.

I certainly didn't need to meet a giant on this trip, so I moved as quietly as I could manage, and hoped we would be there very quickly.

Carefully and quietly, we made our way down the steep embankment towards the rushing water that was anything but peaceful. The water foamed and appeared to have multiple currents running in different directions. It was no wonder it sounded so violent—it *was* violent. The fact that Melinoe and Grace had made it this far said great things about Mel's ability to captain a boat.

When I saw the boat, my heart nearly jumped out of my chest. The water was calmer beneath the bridge, and I had no doubt my friends had used some kind of trick to be able to drop anchor here and stay a while without being swept away. The vessel wasn't large enough to be considered a ship, although it was certainly larger than your average fishing boat.

The wood of the boat was glossy and black, with a carving of a ghost at the front to peer out over the water. The eyes weren't black, though, they were little glinting bits of silver. I recalled Hades's mirrored eyes and shivered. Even if he was only Melinoe's stepfather, I finally caught a family resemblance.

"I'll go a little ahead and let them know you are with me," the ghost said.

I nodded, but felt torn between running towards the boat and yelling for Grace, and standing there shaking until she came to me and told me she didn't hate me.

I barely saw the ghost move as he boarded the boat, just little fuzzy movements that I wouldn't even have noticed if I hadn't been looking for them. I saw a small door open, and watched as Melinoe walked out onto the deck and looked out in the direction I was standing. Her black fingertips and hands were invisible on the side of the boat, as if she was simply a part of it, or as if it was part of her.

She didn't smile or seem overly excited to see me, but she motioned for me to come aboard.

Walking quickly but cautiously, I crossed what was left of the space between us. I didn't even look at the ground, but only where I was headed. I heard the pitch change as my boots hit the wood of the boat's ramp, and had to slow my pace because it was so steep.

At the top of the ramp, there was a gap where I would have to take a very large step or small hop to get across, otherwise risking an injured or broken leg if I fell. Thankfully, it wasn't wide enough for me to fall through completely. I paused so I could get my bearings before jumping, and a hand extended to me to help me across.

The hand wasn't Melinoe's: the skin was much too fair, and it wasn't delicate enough to be Grace's. It was a hand I recognized, though. It was big and calloused, and had made me feel safe more times than I could count.

I took the hand and jumped across the gap, landing in Soren's arms, and started to cry.

CHAPTER SEVENTEEN

Minutes later, I was still crying to the point that I couldn't catch my breath, and he was still holding me just as tightly. I could hear his own sniffs, and felt a few hot tears touch my skin that had just run down his face.

He stroked my hair and kissed the top of my head, whispering something I couldn't quite make out over my sobs.

"Yeah yeah, very touching, but I want my turn too," Grace's voice interrupted.

I pulled back from Soren and wiped my face on my sleeve as I turned to her.

I saw tear stains down her face through her makeup on the side where she still had an eye. I held out my arms to her, and she came to me and hugged me.

"Why am I always looking for you?" she asked with a sigh.

"I'm just so glad you do," I told her.

Grace released me from our embrace and took Melinoe's hand in her own. "She helped a lot."

I hugged Melinoe next, which seemed to catch her off guard because I felt her body tense, but then she relaxed after a moment. "Thank you," I told her.

"I needed an adventure anyway," she said.

Soren moved to be at my side and wrapped his arm around my waist, as if he we wasn't ever going to allow any distance between us from now on. I was fine with that, and placed my hand over his.

"Come inside and fill us in," Grace urged.

I followed my friends through the little door, and was surprised by how much room there was. Two small, but cozy, couches lined the walls, and then there was another door that I assumed led into the sleeping and kitchen quarters.

I took a seat beside Soren on one of the couches, and Melinoe and Grace took the other opposite us.

"I probably already know the answer to this," said Grace, "but is there any chance we can take you home with us?"

I dropped my head and shook it. "I don't think so."

Soren squeezed my hand and I looked at my friends. "Is there any chance you can stay?"

Melinoe shook her head. "This isn't the place for us, and as we discovered when we first arrived, Grace can't even leave the ship in this land.

I furrowed my brow. "What do you mean?"

"I tried, but the minute my feet touched the ground I became violently ill. Apparently vampires are less than welcome in this part of the underworld," she sighed.

"Oh," I said, not sure what I could add.

"I can travel here," said Soren. "I'd like to stay a while, if you want me to."

I smiled. "As long as you want." Then I asked, "How are things back in the other underworld? How is everyone?"

"Boude and Andreas suspected as much about not being able to freely roam here, and Andreas didn't seem to be a fan of traveling by water, so they sent letters in case we found you. They are... the same as always," Grace laughed.

"How is Ray, and Billy?" I couldn't ask my questions fast enough. "I still feel terrible I didn't get to tell Ray goodbye."

"He understood the situation, but said you had been dealt the short end of the stick your whole life, and now death. But he said he knew you'd make the best of things and make him proud. He met a nice feisty lady named Linette, and they went off together to see where they wanted to move on to the next. They were playing around with the idea of becoming spirit guides. I think that would be a brilliant plan for Ray, but I think Linette might be a bad influence on whoever she was supposed to guide," Soren chuckled.

"Linette?" I asked. "Did she have short reddish-brown hair, and like to drink?"

Soren raised an eyebrow and nodded, "Yes. Did you know her?"

"I reaped her," I laughed. "I bet they were something to see together." I smiled at the thought, trying not to think about the fact that I'd never see the dad who raised me again.

"Billy?" I asked again.

"He and Margaret are married," Soren smiled.

"Oh yay! I'm so happy for them," I sighed contentedly.

"Me too," he said, but not with the full level of excitement that my own voice had held.

I turned to Grace and Melinoe. "How have your adventures around the world and underworld gone?"

"It was pretty exciting, until we got back and you were gone. We've spent the last year looking for you. Finding you was the hardest thing we've done. We would have never found you if you hadn't sent that squirrel to Soren," Grace remarked.

I smiled. *Furry messenger.*

"Can you stay on the ship with us, at least for tonight?" Grace pleaded.

"I'd love to, even more than you know, but I don't think I should. I'm the ruler of my own little area now, and I'm still working out the kinks," I said.

"How are you still getting things in order when you've been here so long?" Soren asked.

I felt my face flush—time to confess my mistake. "Yeah, so the Norns basically plopped me here and said, 'make things the way you want,' so I did. I created my own little underworld, complete with day and night. They didn't tell me that my standards of time would be different than everywhere else. By my time, I've only been here a few days."

"That explains why we didn't hear from you. You didn't know how much time was passing." Soren patted my leg to comfort me.

"I would have never intentionally stayed away from any of you, especially for so long. You know that," I said.

He kissed me on the cheek.

I wanted to hear all of the details of everything I had missed, but I could feel myself being pulled, almost physically, back to Helheim. My heart broke at the thought of saying goodbye to Grace again, but at least they now knew how to get back to me, and that I could see them again. And best of all, Soren was staying for a while.

Grace was looking paler by the minute, and I knew that even staying here on the water was still draining her somehow. I went to be beside her on the couch and wrapped my arms around her. "You have no idea how happy I am to see you and know that you are doing well. I'll look into finding a remedy for you when you are here so you can stay longer, and I'll be more diligent about sending messages by squirrel," I giggled.

Grace hugged me back, but her usual bubbly enthusiasm was low. Her eye was droopy, and she seemed to have trouble lifting her arms.

I turned to Melinoe. "This will pass when you leave, right?"

"It will—it goes away when we're moving. She will be fine," Melinoe assured me.

I nodded, "Get her out of here." I stood, as did Mel, so she could proceed to get the vessel moving.

I hugged Melinoe again and said, "Thank you for taking care of her. She's very special."

"It's my pleasure," she said.

Hand in hand, Soren and I left the boat and began making our way towards Helheim.

CHAPTER EIGHTEEN

I WAS BEYOND EXCITED TO BRING SOREN BACK TO my territory and show him my work and my people. I hoped he would want to stay a long time, maybe even forever. He'd probably miss Billy though, and his reaping work. I couldn't blame him if that was the case.

We stole glances of one another as we walked, and for some reason my mind was blank on subjects to talk about. I felt nervous around him. So much must have happened since the last time I saw him, and I could feel that distance. Yet it was so strange, because for me, it didn't seem like that long ago.

Even though the conversation was lacking, it felt wonderful to have my hand back in his once again and just be in his presence.

The air was cool and it was growing darker as we walked. I couldn't believe I had already been gone the whole day. In the distance I saw the faint shadow that I knew must be the wall that surrounded Helheim.

"We're not far," I told Soren. I didn't try to hide my enthusiasm.

"What's that?" he asked, and nodded ahead of us.

"The wall of bodies?" I chuckled. I knew Soren

would be one of the few people who would appreciate the morbid structure as much as I did.

He raised an eyebrow at me. "Bodies?" he questioned.

I started to explain the purpose of the wall, but about that time I saw the shadow of a person move away from it—only, they were taller than the wall itself: a giant.

"Umm, we should hide," I quickly suggested.

Soren was being as still as a statue. "We're out in the open. There's nothing to hide behind."

I stood motionless as his side. Every fantasy movie I had ever seen played through my head, where giants and ogres picked up the minuscule little humans and took a bite out of them. Sure, I had faced zombies and crazed vampires and demons, but there was something about being confronted with a being that could crush half your body by accidentally stepping on you that was freaking me out more than I could express.

I considered creating something for us to hide under or behind, but figured it would probably just make us stand out a lot more, if some kind of structure just suddenly appeared where there wasn't one before.

"What should we do?" I asked Soren, panic swelling up in me to the point I was fighting the urge to run away and scream.

"This is your territory, remember. I don't know anything about this part of the underworld," he said.

"Shit," I said softly. I didn't know much about it either. "This," I rolled my eyes around so I didn't wave my hands, "isn't part of my territory. My area is Helheim, inside that wall. I don't know anything about out here."

About that time we noticed the huge shadow was getting even bigger as it made its way towards us.

It was nearly dark, but not so dark that there could be any chance that we weren't seen by the giant.

Soren's hands clenched at his sides and he bent his knees slightly to brace for impact or prepare to launch himself into an attack. I took a deep breath and stiffened my spine, but instead of standing still, I moved forward towards the giant lumbering towards us.

"Helena!" Soren growled my name as though it was an order, but I ignored him.

The closer I walked to the giant, the more afraid I was; but instead of cowering, I forced myself to hold my head higher, as if I were wearing a strong and elegant crown that I couldn't allow to slip.

The very last of the light was fading, and within minutes darkness would be on us. I had to stand a little way back, so that the giant could see me without risking being stepped on.

"You there!" I called in my strongest, loudest voice. "What are you doing peeking around my wall?"

The giant wasn't ugly or uncouth, as books and movies had led me to believe. He was actually quite handsome, just nearly eight times the size of a normal man. I didn't even come up to his knee.

He eyed me and gave me a gentle smile. "I sometimes come to the edge of your wall to watch the battles, and sometimes to talk to a friend of mine. I'm sorry if that isn't allowed, Your Highness. I'll stop if you wish it."

"Who is your friend?" I asked. I immediately liked the giant upon speaking with him.

"Baldur, the one you left in charge. He was asking if I had seen you on your journey."

I smiled, "You are welcome to watch the battles and training over the wall, and to visit with Baldur whenever you wish. What is your name, so that I might tell Baldur that I have met a friend of his?"

"I am Hugi," he said. I was surprised how soothing I found the rumble of his voice. It sounded like distant thunder as you fell asleep at night.

"It's been a pleasure meeting you, Hugi. You might want to tell your friend Baldur to stop joking about giants eating dogs," I laughed.

The giant nodded and smiled, but had a very confused look in his eyes that made me regret saying anything. Thankfully, he changed the subject.

"Who is your little angry looking friend?"

I turned to see Soren still in position to fight, and he did indeed look angry. I burst out laughing at the idea of anyone calling Soren "little," but to the giant I guess he was. Soren was one of the biggest men I'd ever been around, and that was one of the reasons I always felt so safe around him.

"He's friendly," I called to Soren, who only slightly relaxed in his tenseness as he walked over to me.

"Soren, this is Hugi. He's a friendly giant."

Hugi smiled proudly.

Soren approached the giant. "You can understand my hesitation I hope," he said, and extended a hand to the giant. I was curious to see how that handshake was going to work.

The giant leaned forward and held his finger out to Soren. Soren laid the palm of his hand over the tip of Hugi's finger, and they smiled at each other.

"Well it's nice to meet you both, but I need to be off. I have things I must do. I hope to see you again sometime, Queen Hel," Hugi said.

"And I you," I told him.

Then in the blink of an eye, Hugi ran out of sight, creating a strong enough wind that I held onto Soren's arm to avoid being blown over.

I wasn't sure what to say about my first experience meeting a giant, and then watching him run lightning-fast across the terrain. However Soren had specific words on the subject.

"Well that was fucking terrifying."

CHAPTER NINETEEN

WITH THE "SPEED-RACING" GIANT BEHIND US, SOREN and I were free to continue making our way toward the wall.

As we approached the large structure that had been built of death, I saw him regard it with fascination and appreciation, just as I had done.

"Where did they get the bones?" he asked.

"No idea, and I don't have any desire to ask the Norns," I said, rolling my eyes. I had a lot of resentment towards them, for valid reasons.

"I wonder how many bodies are in there," he mused.

I stared at the wall again too. It would be one of those things you could look at forever and always find new things to see. "I wonder what happened to the souls. Maybe these are the bones of the people who are in Helheim."

"So you think you have their souls, and their bones protect where they are spending their eternity?" Soren asked.

"I think that would be kind of romantic, don't you?"

Soren smiled and ducked his head, like he wasn't sure how to respond to me. "I think your idea of romance has darkened over the years."

I cringed at his words. He was really feeling our time apart. With a touch, I opened a hole in the wall and stepped through, turning to close the gap once Soren stepped through as well. I made sure we were nowhere near the gate so we didn't attract attention.

I took his hand in mine and gave it a gentle squeeze. "Is anyone waiting for you back at home?" I couldn't stand not knowing if there had been someone else.

"Helena, you know me. It is rare for anyone to claim my attention, and you have held mine since nearly the moment we met. What about you? Do you have another Viking in your life?" he teased.

My mind replayed my conversations and close encounters with Baldur. I was so glad that I hadn't given into my desire. "No. I've only been here a couple of days, remember?"

"I'm sorry if I seem distant," he said, and used his free hand to rub the back of his head. "I can't imagine how strange that must be for you—for it to have only been a few days for you, and so long for me. Yet so much has happened for both of us in that time."

"It is strange for both of us. Do you want to be here with me—are you seeing if things feel the same? Or do you feel obligated?" I asked. Obligated. That word made my teeth clench. I couldn't bear the thought of someone feeling obligated to do anything for me to spare my feelings, or life, or what-have-you. If that's how he felt, I'd just turn around and escort him right back to the river. Which brought another issue to mind, but that could wait a moment.

"Of course I don't feel obligated to stay. I missed you, Helena. You are my love—but you can't expect us to step right back into the role we were playing before you left."

"I know, it will all take some adjustments," I agreed.

"Don't doubt that I am very glad to have you back in my arms." He pulled me in for another kiss.

"Really? You haven't had sex with anyone?" I asked.

"Why do you find that hard to believe? I hadn't been with anyone since Eira when we came together," he reminded me.

"I know, but you're just so good at it. It seems wasteful for you not to have sex with someone."

He shook his head at me, as he often did. "It is only wasteful if I'm having sex with someone I don't want to be with, and you are the only one I wanted."

I kissed him hard and wrapped my arms around his neck, pressing my body against his. "I can't wait for you to see my new bedroom."

A small cough to get our attention sounded behind us, and I turned. A young woman was standing there. "So sorry to bother you, Queen Hel, but I just wanted to make sure you were OK."

I smiled at her. "I'm fine, thank you for checking on me though."

The young woman had a shield at her side and a small dagger on her belt. She was in training. She gave Soren a disapproving look, but conceded and walked away. I was willing to bet she hadn't always been treated kindly by men.

"It seems you have spies everywhere," said Soren as he watched her walk away.

"So it seems," I agreed.

"Now, about showing me that bedroom," he said.

CHAPTER TWENTY

I SAW SOREN'S EYES GROW WIDE AS WE WALKED around Helheim, making our way towards the dining hall. He paused to watch the people training with axes and other various weapons. One moment they were screaming at each other in what could have been mistaken for fits of pure rage, and the next they were picking themselves up off the ground, laughing about what a good hit that had been. He passed by the older folks who were working in the garden, and rested his hands on the wooden fence the people had built.

"I know you haven't seen everything, but what do you think so far?" I asked, coming to stand beside him.

"I think it's the closest place to home and heaven that I've ever been," he said, and pulled me in against his body.

I grinned, feeling more proud of myself than I had in a very long time. "Are you hungry?" I asked.

"Always."

One of the older guards opened the door to the dining hall, and the roar of voices and laughter rushed at us, along with the heat from the fireplaces that had been well stocked with chopped wood.

I saw a look of utter excitement cross Soren's face. A man who looked to be about Soren's age with a fuzzy red beard was walking by, and he handed Soren a mug of beer.

"Welcome, brother!" the bearded man said, and patted Soren on the shoulder.

Soren took a long swig of the beer and wiped his face with his hand.

"I thought you had left us for good, so I had them declare me king!" a loud and jovial voice called from my right.

I rolled my eyes at Baldr. "Is that why you asked Hugi to keep an eye out for me?"

"You met my giant friend, huh? He's a nice guy, but a little slow."

"Ha!" Soren said in reply.

Baldur stepped over and extended a hand to the other man. "The name is Baldur. You must be Soren. Hel has told me all about you."

Soren shook the man's hand and smiled at me.

"Where is my dog?" I asked Baldur, hand on my hips as I looked around impatiently.

"Couldn't drag him off your bed since I brought him back this morning. I've checked on him a few times though, and I took him a bone."

"Thank you," I said. "Anything else I need to know about?"

Baldur brushed his hair back from his shoulders and scratched his scruffy beard. I was very aware of how attracted I was to him, which made me super uncomfortable while standing next to Soren. Baldur was some sort of golden god, and Soren was sexy as hell, but his was a hardened kind of warrior. Baldur had something that Soren didn't, or maybe he had just lost it long ago through the hardships he had endured.

He hesitated too long, so I asked again. "What aren't you telling me?"

"The women with infants and small children are wondering if you're going to help them," he said quickly as if he was trying to get it over with.

"Ugh, I know. That will be my full focus tomorrow. I'll have an answer for them by tomorrow night," I sighed, "even if I have to visit the Norns."

Baldur nodded. "I told them I was certain you hadn't forgotten. Well, I'll get out of your way so the two of you can catch up. There are two seats and plates at the end of the table for you both. Enjoy your dinner, and get some rest."

There was the tiniest bit of disappointment in Baldur's eyes. I knew instinctively the two place settings he had laid out weren't for Soren and me, but for himself and me. I thought of the awkwardness between me and Soren caused by all of this, and for just a split second wished that it was Baldur I would be dining with. Baldur walked away, no obvious trace of anything wrong in his demeanor as he called to another friend and took a seat beside him. Everyone at the table grinned as Baldur joined them. It was obvious he was as well loved in the underworld as he had been in life.

"Shall we eat?" Soren's voice made me jump, and I realized I had been staring at Baldur. *Yeah, I need to stop this real fast.*

"Absolutely," I said, and took his hand in mine once more.

We sat down at the table and ate the dinner before

us. The food was warm and nourishing after having traveled all day. The conversation, however, was still on the dry side. In an attempt to lessen the tension, I placed my hand on his thigh and traced lines back and forth. I was still attracted to Soren, and I loved him—I should be tearing his clothes off. Instead, the fact that my touch was an effort, instead of effort*less*, left a part of me feeling empty. So I did the only thing I could think of that might help: I drank—a lot.

Soren helped me to my bedroom, which I insisted was unnecessary. I wasn't *that* drunk. I could walk, I just had to stop now and then to rest against a wall. Since the distance from the dining hall to my bedroom wasn't that far, maybe I was slightly inebriated.

I opened the door to my room and was nearly knocked down by an even bigger Garmr. Barely inside the door, I sat on the floor and wrapped my arms around the big dog, letting him give me slobbery kisses and nuzzles.

"Did you miss me?" I cooed. "Did my wittle baby miss his mommy?"

Soren's laughter wasn't subtle as he watched me. "He's a beauty. Is he grown?"

I shrugged and rubbed the dog's belly. "I have no idea."

Soren stepped forward to pet the hellhound and the dog jumped up and pulled back its head. He didn't growl or show aggression, or even fear. He simply acted like he didn't want Soren to touch him.

"Garmr, it's OK. Soren is our buddy," I reassured the dog.

He hesitantly stretched his long nose out and sniffed Soren's hand, and then backed away, going to the door and whining to be let out.

"Just let him out," I said to Soren. "He's probably going to go play now that he knows I'm back." It would have taken me far too much effort to stand and open the door while the room was still spinning.

Soren opened the door and the dog ran out into the building. I knew everyone would look out for him, so I wasn't worried about keeping him with me. Besides, things were probably going to get sexy in here, and I didn't need a cold nose in an unexpected place.

A hand extended to me where I had slumped to the floor, and I instinctively took it. Soren pulled me up onto my feet and brushed my hair back from my face where it had slipped out of my bun. I wasn't looking him in the eyes, and even the alcohol coursing through me wasn't enough to keep me from being nervous.

"Why are you acting as though you don't know me?" Soren asked, and a small part of my heart broke. That was the problem: it was only a small part of my heart.

I forced myself to look him in the eyes and answer him honestly. "I don't know. I think I lost something when I had to leave our underworld. I don't feel calloused, and I still care deeply for everyone, but it's like I'm experiencing my emotions through a filter. The bad things don't hurt as much, but the good things don't feel as good either."

Soren hugged me, and I thought that I should probably be crying at all of this, but I didn't need to.

"May I sleep in here?" he asked.

"Of course. You know you don't have to ask," I told him.

"I did have to ask. Are you certain you want me in

your bed? I'm not expecting sex."

I was considering whether or not I wanted sex, which was shocking, since I was always up for sex.

I knew Soren would be able to sense my hesitation—I mean, any hesitation at all would have given me away to someone who knew me as well as he did. An actual pause was certain to make him doubt my feelings.

"Cuddling, and see where things go from there?" I asked.

Soren kissed me on the head. "Whatever you want."

CHAPTER
TWENTY-ONE

I CHANGED INTO A NIGHTGOWN AND TOSSED Soren a pair of soft pants to sleep in. We had never slept beside one another in clothing. Maybe I was just making things more awkward.

Soren pulled the blankets and furs down so that we could get into bed. I lowered the burn of the fire to a soft glow and laid down beside him. I wiggled and moved around, trying to get comfortable and decide what position I should be in. Did I want to face him, the ceiling, or the wall?

He put his hand on my shoulder, and I turned on my side to look at him. He smiled at me and asked, "Helena, do you want me to sleep somewhere else?"

My mind drifted back to the first night Raphael stayed with me and asked me nearly the same question. That night I had been trying my best to inch closer to him without obviously throwing myself on top of him. The memory made me smile; it had been a while since I'd thought of Raphael.

I looked at Soren—really looked at him: his gray eyes and blond hair and beard against his fair complexion. I thought of all the times we had shared together. His was the first face that I saw when I opened my eyes in the underworld, and he had picked me up (literally) when I thought that I no longer had the strength to go on. When the Norns had forced me to come here, I'd been sure that he was gone from me forever. How many people got this kind of chance?

My lips curled into a grin as I looked at him, and I wrapped my hand around his.

"You never fail to find ways to amaze me," he said. "What you have created here for yourself is beyond anything I could have imagined."

I felt the warm dampness of happy tears in my eyes and tried to ignore them, but he went on.

"What you're doing for the souls that come to you— giving them purpose and letting them continue to live... this is more than anyone could hope to get when they die."

A tear rolled down my cheek, and I quickly wiped it away and pretended it had never happened.

"Are you OK? Are you happy here?" he asked me.

"I miss everyone, more than I can begin to explain. You, Grace, Billy, Ray, the vampires—all of you are so important to me. Baldur is really the only friend I've made here, and he doesn't hold a candle to all of you. If I could go home with you and know the souls here would be OK, I would in a heartbeat," I confessed.

Soren kissed me. His lips pressed hard against mine, and I felt his tongue at my mouth, urging it to open. I didn't feel the need to hesitate this time. The warmth of his mouth against mine made me shiver and move in closer to him. He pulled away, though, breaking the kiss before I was ready, and I whimpered.

"I'll stay," he said.

I felt my brows furrow, and asked, "What do you mean? For how long?"

"As long as you want, Helena. Even forever." He leaned in to kiss me again.

This time I pulled back before his lips could meet mine. "Soren, are you sure? What about reaping? What about Billy?"

"I didn't want to upset you, but things back at home aren't the same. I don't need to be there anymore," he said, and I could see the mention of it had made him uncomfortable.

I sat up in the bed; this wasn't a conversation to have while lying down. "What do you mean? How are things different?"

Soren sat up as well. The mood had suddenly shifted. "Almost everyone is gone. Ray left to be a spirit guide with Linette. Billy and Margaret got married, and when their time was served they went to heaven. After that, there was only one other reaper besides myself, and when it came time to have my watch reset, I told them I didn't want to be a reaper anymore. You know my time was up a long time ago, but I didn't know what else I wanted to do or where to go. I didn't want to be a reaper without you or Billy there."

I sighed, "So even if I could find a way back, nothing would be the same?"

"Well, Andreas is the same," Soren said with a smile.

I couldn't help the laugh that escaped my lips. "Of course he is. What about Boude?"

"Boude is well. He's been working for Hades and Persephone—some kind of plan to blend the vampires and human souls a little more." He shrugged as if he didn't know that much about it.

"Hmm," I said, wondering what that could be about, and then I turned my attention back to Soren. My head was still spinning, in part from the alcohol, and in part from all the new information I had just learned. I couldn't fathom how different things were now. Soren and Billy weren't reapers anymore. Everyone was gone, or had new jobs. I was a queen with my own kingdom. How was death so much crazier than life?

All of the same thoughts seemed to be on rotation through my mind, and I needed them to stop. I got up on my knees and moved in closer to Soren. My hair fell around us in waves as I leaned over him, and then down to kiss his lips.

I kissed him ever so lightly at first, and then swept my tongue across his lips and into his mouth. Before he could respond, I broke the kiss, and kissed across his cheek and over to his ear, where I traced my tongue along the edge, and then gently nibbled at his earlobe.

Soren made a noise that sounded almost like an expression of pain—which gave me all the incentive I needed to keep going. I was at a slightly awkward angle, so I moved to him. Once I settled into a better position I realized why the noises he was making sounded so desperate. He was pressed rock hard against my leg. Feeling him so ready to go, so eager, and knowing how long he had waited for me was all that I had needed.

I knew what Soren liked. I knew that he enjoyed sex just as much as me, whether it was hard or gentle. But I also knew that, just like me... he liked it rough.

While one hand reached down to rub the length of him over the pants he was wearing, my other hand rested on his shoulder, where I dug my nails into the bare flesh. I sucked on his earlobe once more, and bit just hard enough to leave teeth marks.

"Fuck, Helena," he half growled, half gasped.

The time that had passed didn't matter anymore. This was what mattered: that we knew each other—enjoyed each other.

I began to tease once more, kissing, biting, and scratching lines that left red welts all down his chest.

"Helena," he breathed, sounding a little more desperate than he had moments ago.

I released the skin I had between my teeth and looked up at him. "Yes?" I asked.

He watched me and breathed heavily, as if he had been running. "Enough," he finally said.

"Is it too much?" I asked, half teasing.

He slowly shook his head no, and I gave him a salacious grin. "So you want me to keep going?"

"You're only making it worse for yourself," he said. His breathing was still labored but the look in his eye now was not one of surrender. He was turning the tables on me again, as he was so fond of doing.

"What do you mean?" I asked.

"Getting me this hard," he looked down where his erection was strained against his pants, "after all this time of being without you? Do you really think I'll be able to control myself and go easy on you?"

I was suddenly hesitant to keep going with my slow, teasing torture. My eyes widened at his words, and as I was still processing them, he moved towards me and wrapped his hand in my hair, pulling my neck and head back.

"Oww," I whined, but not entirely in a bad way.

He held onto my hair as he moved himself out from

under me and made his way behind me. He put a hand between my shoulders and pushed me down onto the bed so that my ass was still in the air. I felt his hand start to push my nightgown up, but then he stopped and pulled me back up by my hair.

"No, not like this. I need to look into your eyes. Don't think it'll be easy, though."

I felt a jolt of electricity surge through my body, stronger in particular areas. I moved to take off my nightgown, and he let me. I lay on the bed, naked below him, and he took his own pants off. I was very aware of how long it felt like it had been since I had seen him naked, and I couldn't wait to feel him inside me. Even if it was going to hurt a little to start with, that was part of the pleasure with Soren. With him, I needed that little bit of pain—it seemed to be one of the few things in the world that took away the bad thoughts and feelings that I dwelled on.

"Legs by your ears," he ordered, and I did as he asked, even though it left me feeling much too exposed.

He kissed me and ran a finger along the most delicate part of me to make sure that I was wet enough for what he wanted to do. After all, he wasn't trying to actually injure me.

I felt him hard and ready, pressed against my opening. He was waiting for just the right moment. I tensed up waiting for it, and he felt me.

"Relax," he said, and grinned at me.

I smiled back at him and exhaled, consciously relaxing my muscles. He plunged himself inside of me as deep and hard as he could manage on that first single thrust.

I screamed. The element of pleasure had been a tiny one, but he was moving now and my body was already adapting. He would let my pleasure build until I was almost ready to orgasm, and then slam into me again, hard enough to make me cry out in pain that was becoming more and more blurred with pleasure.

"I'm going to go faster and harder. Can you go when I do?" he asked.

Unable to speak, I just nodded. He thrust in and out of me hard and fast, but was careful not to change his rhythm so that I wouldn't lose my orgasm this time.

As the pressure kept building, I dug my nails into his back and let my legs rest on his shoulders. My hips were going to hurt tomorrow. The orgasm washed over me, and I screamed as I wrapped my body around his. He came seconds after I did, and held onto me with every fiber of his being.

We collapsed, with him still on top of me, and my legs and arms wrapped all around him. After a moment, he said, "I'll move over, so you can breathe."

Still panting, I held him even tighter and said, "Don't you dare."

CHAPTER
TWENTY-TWO

SOREN AND I SLEPT, ONLY UNTANGLING OURSELVES at some point during the night in our sleep. Even then, we were still touching.

We woke up the next morning to Garmr barking at my door. I wrapped a blanket around me and shuffled to the door. When I opened it, Garmr ran in and jumped onto the bed, not realizing that he leapt onto a sleeping man.

Soren made an, "Oomph," kind of sound as the giant dog landed on him, and then patted the dog's head and tried to settle back down to sleep.

Garmr didn't reject Soren's affections, but he didn't wag his tail or act very excited about it either. So strange.

I crawled back into bed, but my rest was short-lived. Soon a knock came from the door, and I knew it was time to get up and get to work.

"Yes?" I called, still warm beneath the covers and cuddled up to Soren and Garmr.

"Sorry to disturb you. I just made some fresh bread and thought you might want some before it's all eaten in the hall," a sweet voice answered from behind the door.

I looked at Soren and he knew our alone time was over. He smiled at me though, and said, "Fresh bread does sound pretty nice."

I had to admit my stomach growling too. "Be right there."

I tried to be subtle while I thought up clothes for Soren, and then pulled them out of the drawer. He watched, but didn't ask any questions. Instead of using it like a cool party trick—"Hey, everyone! Look what I can create!"—it just made me feel like a bit of a freak, albeit, a grateful one. For myself I picked out a simple pair of leather pants to wear with a soft sweater and boots. I left my hair down and simply pulled the top strands back so that it was out of my face.

We entered the dining hall and took a seat. The smell of the fresh bread was heavenly, and the fig preserves were delicious. I was so distracted by my hunger and the yummy food in front of me that I hadn't realized there were no other men in the dining hall besides Soren.

The children were running around playing, and the mom's who stayed in the living quarters of the hall were busy eating or doing their daily tasks; but they all kept eyeing me, and steadily becoming more obvious about it. I didn't feel threatened. They were mothers: mothers of children that needed help. And like it or not, I was the person who could give them answers.

When they noticed that I was watching them, they all tried to busy themselves as if they were afraid of angering me. I smiled gently at them, stood from the table, and said, "Ladies." I watched as they all turned to face me before continuing, "I assure you, I have not forgotten your needs. I completely understand this is an urgent matter, and I assure you that I will find out what should be done. Please keep in mind, I've never taken care of others on this level. I'm learning as we go. You can always approach me about your needs."

Several of the women nearby bowed their heads and thanked me. I recalled my own awkward curtsy to Persephone. It felt wrong for people to have so much faith in me. I wasn't really deserving of this. After all, I had been thrown in this position without really wanting it.

The look on my face must have shown my concern because Soren put his hand over mine and patted it.

"So you can hang around here today and explore, or come with me to see the Norns," I told Soren.

He wrinkled his nose, making a face of disgust. "I will, of course, go with you to see the Norns..." he trailed off. "If you want me to."

I shook my head and said, "That's not necessary. I don't really want to take you around them in case they decide to be mean again and take you away from me." I leaned over and kissed him on the cheek. "You should wander around and meet everyone. If you're going to stay a while, you should find something to do that you would enjoy."

Soren stroked his beard and smiled, he looked happy. "How long do you think you'll be gone?" he asked.

"No clue, but I have to get this sorted out. I'll find you when I get back."

"That's fine," he said, and picked up another piece of bread from the table.

I kissed him once more and headed out the door of the hall with Garmr by my side. It was sunny outside, but a little on the chilly side. It was tempting to change the weather to my liking daily, since it tended to run cool here. The irony of it being "a cold day in Hel" wasn't lost on me. I wrapped my sweater around my body more tightly and began walking towards the tree. I waved at the people I passed, and watched the women practice fighting alongside the men. Since I was trying to answer requests today, I recalled the woman asking me for horses. Out in the distant field, I imagined horses grazing and galloping through the hills. When I blinked again they were there.

I didn't say anything to anyone. I kept walking, and soon I heard shouting and laughter from everyone yelling to one another, "Look! Horses!"

I made up my mind to be a little more patient at the tree this time. Even if it took the Norns a while to get here, I needed their help and I wouldn't risk going back to those mothers without some kind of answer.

After I knocked on the root and called out to them I sat down and waited. It wasn't long until one of them was standing in front of me.

"Hel," she greeted me.

"I'm sorry. I don't know which one you are," I admitted, wishing I had been able to greet her by name.

"I am Skuld," she answered, and didn't look too annoyed that I didn't know her.

"Don't the three of you always travel together?" I asked.

"Most of the time, yes; but not always. What do you need?" Skuld didn't seem as though she was trying to be rude, she just seemed to be in a hurry.

"There are mothers in Hel with their babies and small children. The young ones can't grow and aren't fulfilling their soul's purpose. What do I do with them?" I asked.

"It sounds like you genuinely care what happens to them."

Her statement caught me off guard. "What do you mean? Of course I care about them," I said defensively.

"You just seemed so unhappy about being given this position," she shrugged and and curled a piece of brittle, wispy hair around her finger. The Norns were such odd... things. Sometimes they appeared so lovely and alive, and at another moment they appeared withered and dry like mummies. It was as if they were the embodiment of both life and death, swapping back and forth.

"Just because I was happy and you dragged me away from my friends doesn't mean that I would let others suffer. I'm here to do a job. I was raised to think that you should always do your best, whether you're digging graves or running an afterlife," I answered in a matter of fact tone of voice.

"We chose well when we chose you for this position," Skuld smirked.

I shrugged. I still didn't really want this job, but I was glad I was good at it. "So how do we help them? Their souls have purpose too, right? How are they to fulfill it if they are staying in child form? Am I not doing something that I'm supposed to?"

Skuld placed a bony finger to her plump red lips. "It

has changed throughout the centuries. We usually have someone to collect the children and care for them or see that they move on. I guess we didn't realize we didn't have someone filling that position at the moment. I'll send someone," she answered as casually as if she was planning to send someone to pick up a package.

"When?" I asked. For all I knew it would be ages.

"By your time it would be tomorrow. Be certain to tell the children's mothers to be ready to say goodbye."

I swallowed hard. I knew that was going to be part of it, and even though I didn't have a child to give up, I couldn't imagine how hard it would be for these women to turn over their kids and know they would never see them again. "OK," I said.

"Will there be anything else?" Skuld asked.

I thought for a moment, but shook my head. "No. Thank you. That's all I needed."

"Very well. We are pleased with your work—and tell Soren that I said hello." She grinned.

I felt anger rise up my face. "Are you going to make him leave? His time is up. He chose to be here!" My voice was getting louder as my concern grew.

"Calm yourself. We are not taking Soren. He may stay," she said, dismissing my anger with a wave of her hand.

I sighed and felt some of the tension leave my shoulders. "Thank you."

Skuld pursed her lips and looked like she wanted to say something else to me, but resisted. I probably didn't want to know what it was anyway.

She looked at the dog at my feet and said, "Sweet puppy."

Garmr whimpered as though he had been scolded,

and then Skuld was gone.

I looked at the giant, loyal hellhound at my feet and said, "Yep, she's scary."

CHAPTER
TWENTY-THREE

WE MADE OUR WAY BACK TOWARDS THE VILLAGE, and as we topped the little hill, what I saw below warmed my heart. Dozens of people were riding horses through the fields, others were constructing a barn, and a few men had fashioned harnesses and were leading little children around on the backs of the horses as they walked in circles. The kids were laughing and their little faces were pink from smiling.

Those sweet smiles were bringing so much joy to us it was going to be a shame to see them go, but so far, every day more souls were coming in, and among those were always children.

I sat for a moment on the grassy hilltop and put a hand on Garmr's back. I was impressed with him. Most dogs would have gone wild their first time seeing horses. I expected him to take off running after them, or even to cower behind me, but he just laid calmly at my side and watched all that was going on.

I wondered who the Norns would be sending for the children, and hoped it wasn't someone scary. You just never knew what you were going to get in the afterlife.

The sights of people enjoying themselves was fun to watch, and the best part was when I saw a large blonde man grinning and hammering as another man held a newly built wall in place.

We continued down into the village, and Garmr decided to go explore now that we were closer to the horses. He approached them cautiously, but since there really wasn't a tremendous difference in their sizes, he wasn't too skittish.

Soren was talking with the other men building the stable, and he had a look of contentment on his face that I had rarely seen.

I walked up behind him and said, "Happy looks good on you."

He looked over his shoulder at me and winked, "I haven't felt this good in ages." He puckered his lips for me to move in to kiss him, and I did.

"Did you get your answer from the Norns?" he asked.

"I did. Skuld said she would send someone tomorrow to pick up the children, so they can determine the best course of action."

Soren said, "Well, that's good, I guess."

"Yeah." I replied. I knew we were both thinking the same thing. Something needed to be done, but how could we know if it was the right thing?

"Do you need me for anything?" Soren asked as he positioned the hammer over a nail to start working again.

"No, I need to talk to the mothers and make the rounds, I guess. You can find me later. Keep working," I said.

"See you in a few hours," he said, and resumed

driving the nail into the wooden plank.

Most of the women waiting for an answer had spotted me as I made my way back towards the hall and followed me inside. Once I was sure the majority were assembled, I told them the situation, and dreaded their reactions.

One woman, with long creamy blonde hair the color of fresh butter, smiled and nodded. "Very good. So there is still hope for their souls to move on and experience life. A chance for them to grow."

I was incredibly relieved that at least one of them had taken it so well. I let out a breath I had been holding, and took in a fresh deep breath, causing myself to get light headed from the rush of oxygen. I put my hands down on the table to steady myself and closed my eyes.

"My Queen, are you alright?" Two of the women rushed to my side.

I stood straighter and opened my eyes, the room swayed again. I closed them once more, and the women helped me sit in the chair that was behind me. *How strange,* I thought. *Am I that upset over all of this?*

A glass of water was placed in front of me, along with some sweet fruits that were meant to be served for dessert. I took a sip of the water and picked up a bite of the fruit, but found the overly sugary smelling food repulsive and pushed it away.

The women surrounding me eyed each other with concern, but didn't let me in on the meaning behind their looks.

"I'm fine," I said. "I think I was just so worried about the news I needed to share with you that I nearly made myself sick."

"We knew that letting our babies go would be part of helping them become who they are supposed to be. It's OK, Queen Hel. You only did what we asked," answered a soft voice.

"All of you should be running this place. You're much stronger-willed than I am," I half laughed.

"We each have our own challenges to face," said one that I knew as Alinda. It was usually her who woke me in the morning, and also her who had the smallest baby among all of them.

"This is true. I wouldn't want to trade places with any of us," I laughed.

A woman with black hair put up in an elegant braid placed her hand on her hip and said, "I would trade with Claire. She's been having sex with Baldur."

All of the women burst out into a chorus of "Ooh's and wow's," followed by requests for details.

A plain but very pretty young woman looked like she wanted to hide under a rock, and she was the only one not laughing. I was willing to bet that she was Claire.

Truthfully, when I heard that news a pang of jealousy shot through me. I had absolutely no right to feel that way, and now with Soren here, I certainly shouldn't want Baldur to save himself for me.

Claire's face was red and her eyes shimmered with unshed tears. She seemed frozen in place, afraid to speak and draw more attention to herself. Oh, to be that young again and think having my sex partners aired to people was the worst thing ever.

"Claire, don't ever be embarrassed because you shared a bed with a man of your own choosing, especially one as sexy as Baldur. You don't have to tell us the details, but we are happy for you. Just a little jealous," I winked and gave her a kind smile.

Her posture softened a little.

"You're one to talk about being jealous!" said the woman who had called Claire out. "I saw the man who came out of your room with you this morning. He's worthy of a few jealous looks as well."

Well, I didn't have to wait long to find the town gossip. I would have to watch out for her. "I am very lucky to have Soren," I told her. Then I asked, "So tell us, who is sharing your bed?"

Her smooth persona faltered for a moment, and she muttered as she decided what to say. "Well.. I, umm... I haven't chosen a man here yet. I'm still weighing my options," she finished, seeming pleased with herself for that answer.

"Of course, with so many handsome people to choose from, it does make for a difficult decision. Who are the front runners?" I kept on. I couldn't help it. I just wanted her to feel a bit of the mortification she had cause poor Claire. *Poor Claire, who had kissed and held Baldur...*

All eyes were on the woman now, "Yes, Roma, tell us," the other women urged.

Roma, I'd remember that.

Roma waved her hands and tried to shrug off all of the questions. "Now now, everyone. I'm not one to kiss and tell." It had become pretty apparent to everyone in the room that she was exactly the type to kiss and tell, therefore she was just lying and wasn't kissing anyone.

Alinda put her hand on my shoulder and refilled my glass of water. "Are you feeling any better?"

"Yes," I answered her, "I believe so."

"Perhaps you should go rest for a while. You still look a little pale," she suggested. "I promise I'll come get you if you are needed."

"That's not a bad idea," I told her. I stood again and asked if there were any more questions about the children before I retired.

"So, tomorrow?" one of the mothers asked again, and I couldn't tell if she was excited, or barely holding back her grief.

"Tomorrow," I answered.

CHAPTER
TWENTY-FOUR

IT DIDN'T EVEN OCCUR TO ME THAT IT MIGHT BE A bad idea until after I had already knocked on Baldur's door. Once it did occur to me, it was too late because I had already knocked. I reassured myself that there was no way he was in his room, and that I could walk away with no one being the wiser. I turned on my heel to head back to my own room, where I should have gone in the first place.

My back had just turned toward his door when I heard it open. I wondered if I could quickly duck inside my room, or say that I had seen someone knock and then run away. He might believe it if I said that Claire had done it.

"Hel?" he asked.

I turned around and tried to act casual. "Oh, hey. I didn't think you were in."

"You didn't give me much of a chance to answer," he said. He didn't have a shirt on, and his eyes were heavy with sleep.

Probably because he was up all night with Claire, my brain insisted. But what I said was, "I just stopped by to talk for a minute, and then realized you probably weren't in."

"I'm here," he smiled sleepily and opened the door a bit wider. "Come on in."

Going against all of the better judgement that I had, I walked back to his door and went inside.

I had only seen the other people's living quarters when I first created everything. I had no idea how the individual tenants had set things up.

In Baldur's room, the fireplace was across from his bed instead of at the end like it was in my room. The room was warm and cozy, and his bed was unmade. I wanted to go crawl into it and sleep beside him. I was still feeling tired and not quite myself; sleep sounded so good.

I stood awkwardly just inside the door. There was nowhere to sit besides on the bed, and I was afraid that if any part of me was on the bed, I wouldn't get up, and that could lead to bad things.

"Sorry if I woke you," I said to Baldur.

"I should be up anyway," he said and ran his fingers through his hair. He smoothed out the blanket on the bed and offered me a seat.

"No thanks, I really shouldn't stay long."

"What did you come to talk to me about?" he asked.

That is an excellent question, I thought. I really hadn't planned this out very well. *Why did I want to come and talk to him? Did I even have a reason?*

"I just wanted to let you know that the Norns are sending someone to pick up the children tomorrow. I had a meeting with the mothers, so everyone is aware." *Oh yeah. That's what I needed to tell him.*

His face was serious as he nodded. "It's the best thing for the children, I'm sure. Do you know who they are sending?"

"No. I wish that I did, but Skuld just said that she would have to find someone."

"Thanks for letting me know," said Baldur.

I think he was waiting for me to move towards the door, but I stayed standing where I was. I couldn't tell if he was acting strange, or if it was me... or if it was both of us.

"Was there something else?" he asked.

I fought with myself about whether or not I should mention the awkwardness, and inevitably said something before I made up my mind. "Are we OK? Things feel weird now."

Baldur gave a smile that wasn't about happiness or humor. "We are fine. I'm just dealing with an emotion I haven't felt in a long time."

"What emotion is that?" I asked him.

"Jealousy."

My face flushed and my head spun again. I probably should have taken that nap.

"Jealous? Of Soren and me?" I needed to clarify.

"I thought that I had made my interest in you pretty clear. I understand he is who you want to be with, though. It's fine, I'm just not used to rejection," Baldur said and shrugged.

"Truthfully, if Soren hadn't come back, there might have been something between us. But he is too much a part of who I am to throw it away. Besides, Claire seems pretty smitten with you after your night together." I stopped and waited for him to say something, but he just stared at me, so I went on. "I had to hear all about it from the town gossip, and I admit... I was also a little jealous."

"Claire did spend the night in my room, but beyond kissing, nothing happened."Baldur scratched his head and looked at the floor.

"You two didn't have sex?"

"No. I think she likes me, and maybe some part of her wanted to try, but she wasn't ready. She didn't act like she was enjoying herself, so I didn't push it. She did fall asleep in my bed, though," said Baldur.

"Poor girl. I mean, it's wonderful you didn't take advantage of her, but to be that nervous and then still be treated by everyone as if she had actually done it anyway... I'm not surprised she looked so mortified."

Baldur looked regretful but didn't say anything.

"Can we still be friends?" I asked. "I even think that you and Soren would get along really well, once you know each other."

Baldur held his arms out for a hug and gave me his best smile. "Of course we can. I'll get over it, and I'm sure you're right."

I went to him and he hugged me tightly. Every fiber of my being thrummed as I repeatedly told myself I'd get over this too.

The rest of the day seemed to drag by. I knew I wasn't feeling like myself, but I couldn't place the reason why. There were far too many possibilities; between the kids leaving, that weird sick feeling that I had in the dining hall, and then everything with Baldur, it was no surprise that I was out of sorts.

Dinnertime was approaching, and I'd need to go back into the hall and act like a queen, not like a confused little girl, no matter how much I felt like one.

Hoping it would make me feel a little more centered and human, I curled my hair and put on a little makeup. I wore a long but casual burgundy dress, and a green velvet jacket over it. The jacket was embroidered with flowers the same burgundy as the dress, and my lipstick matched as well. Looking at myself in the mirror, I almost didn't recognize the woman I had become—but I liked her. I wasn't trying to impress anyone this evening. This was all for me, and that was good.

I walked into the dining hall and was met with huge smiling faces and many bows and nods. Nearly everyone remarked on how pretty I looked—which was great, until I caught Baldur watching me, and then saw him look away when he noticed that I'd seen him.

I took a deep breath and walked through the crowd until I spotted Soren. He had been working on the barn all day and was standing with the men he'd been helping.

"There you are," I said as I walked up to him.

"Hey, beautiful," he said and pulled me in for a kiss.

He introduced me to the men who were standing there, and as I said hello to them I was struck by how similar they looked. Not identical, of course, but they could have easily been related.

Soren looked so happy. He tucked me under his arm and held me there like it was where I belonged. I loved seeing him so happy.

The servers began bringing in enormous amounts of food. Some of it I had made sure stayed stocked in the pantry, but other foods people had grown in their gardens. I noticed a lot of the platters contained small finger foods that the children frequently ate and enjoyed, and overheard everyone talking about all of the desserts that had been prepared. I realized that this was a going-away dinner for the kids—well, the ones big enough to eat solid food, anyway.

Soren sat beside me while we ate, and Baldur sat far away. The women that I was getting to know were either sitting near their husbands and lovers, or congregating together. I missed Grace. These women were nice, but I had yet to make a true girlfriend here that I felt I could confide in. I wondered what Grace would think of the Baldur situation.

People frequently went in and out of the dining hall all day long for one reason or another, so I didn't pay much attention to the large doors opening and closing. After all, that was why I had guards.

However, it was unusual for both doors to open, especially all the way. Even though there were windows in the hall, they weren't very large and didn't let in a great deal of light. That, and the fact that Hel was always on the chilly side, were two of the reasons there were always fires going in the fireplaces, and low hanging chandeliers throughout. So when both front doors opened fully, and the remaining bits of sunlight from outside poured into the hall, everyone looked. Through the massive, wide-open doors, came a woman.

CHAPTER
TWENTY-FIVE

HER HAIR DANCED AROUND HER AS SHE ENTERED; it was the color of red autumn leaves in the sun. It didn't remind me of fire, it was far too rich for that, with more facets and highlights than a garnet or ruby. Human women would have killed for a dye job that good.

Her dress was pale blue and corseted under her full breasts. Her skin was pale with rosy undertones, and her smile was gentle and warm.

She moved gracefully through the hall, and stopped to stand amid the tables and rows of people who were now neglecting their dinners to gape openly at her, myself included.

"I am Caireen," she announced in a thick Irish accent, "Goddess of the wee ones."

Still no one moved or said anything. A light tapping on my shoulder caused me to turn and see one of the mothers standing behind me. "She's waiting for you, My Queen."

Shit, that's right. I'm the queen. I stood and moved myself out from the table and toward our guest.

"Welcome, Caireen," I said, and offered her my

hand as I approached.

Caireen took my hand in hers. She didn't shake it, or kiss it, but she simply held it in a friendly comforting way, as you would a nervous child.

"We are very pleased to have you here. As you can see, there are tiny ones here who never had the chance to fulfil their soul's purpose, and I am unable to help them move on. The Norns told me that they would send someone who could help." She probably already knew the situation, but I just felt the need to clarify.

She smiled and said, "That's why I'm here. I'll take the babes with me and get them where they should be going. Are they all ready?"

A mother holding the hand of a little boy who looked to be about one year old stepped forward. "We thought you weren't coming until tomorrow, so we planned an evening of the children's favorite foods and games."

I looked at Caireen. "You are welcome to stay tonight, of course, if you can spare the time."

The goddess looked around the room and nodded. "I could eat," she said.

I invited her to come sit with Soren and me. She filled up her plate, and Soren poured her a glass of mead.

"I have to say, Hel is a much nicer place than I've heard. I was expecting it to be dark, and cold and depressing," said Caireen as she took a bite of bread.

"That is pretty much how it was when I got here," I chuckled.

"Well you've done a beautiful job with things, and your people seem to really like you."

"I try to keep everyone happy and meet their needs,"

I said. "May I ask, where is it that you'll be taking the children? How do their souls move on?"

She sighed as if it was a complex process. "Well in some of the other underworlds, they only go by the paperwork from when the soul was first created. They just reincarnate the soul to give it another chance, and don't take anything else into consideration other than what was first written. I'm hardly so obsessive about that. A child might not have the capability to understand all of its options, but the soul itself does. I put the child into a dreamy kind of sleep and pull out the soul. I tell it what its options are, and release it. From there they find their own way."

"Is it scary for the child?" I asked.

"Heaven's no, Dear. Children love me, and it isn't scary at all for them. Once their soul chooses a direction their body just fades away, since they'll be getting a new one," Caireen answered.

"It's pretty cool to be able to help little ones move on like that," I told her.

"It's pretty cool to get to run your own underworld," she winked.

Normally after dinner, the children played games by themselves while the adults cleaned up or attended to whatever chores they needed to complete for the evening. Tonight, however, everyone got involved in the games.

We fashioned makeshift bowling sets between the rows of tables, and I showed everyone how to play. It was a good thing there weren't many breakables in the hall, since more than one of the men threw the ball like they were at a carnival trying to win a prize.

Caireen took turns playing with the kids, talking with the mothers, and holding the tiny babies. I watched as the moms spoke with her, and saw how they trusted her so instinctively that they handed her their babies to hold while they talked.

I was so glad that she hadn't just come in in a whirlwind and taken the children away—that she stayed and was reassuring everyone that this was the best choice for all involved.

I heard loud voices—adult voices—and looked over to see that a large group of men had taken over a game of bowling when the kids had moved onto something else. I watched a moment and determined that Baldur and Soren were on opposing teams. That probably wasn't good.

Soren had just rolled and had managed to knock over all but two of the pins. Baldur was stepping up now, and turned to Soren and the other men.

I could tell by the way he was trying to hold himself steady that he'd had more than a few drinks this evening.

He said, "I think we should raise the stakes. Winner gets to kiss the queen!"

Soren grinned at Baldur, but not in the friendliest type of way. He looked my direction to see if I was aware of what was going on, and I hoped that I didn't look as horrified as I felt.

"If you win and she'll let you kiss her, that's fine. Just remember, I'm the one taking her to bed tonight," Soren told Baldur, and winked at me.

I appreciated Soren throwing the "if she'll let you"

part in there, but I still wasn't crazy about being their prize.

I walked over to them and nodded for Baldur to take his turn.

The ball rolled down the aisle, and started to drift slightly to the right just as it had when all of the other men had played. The floor wasn't perfectly level, but hey, I had designed this place to live in—it wasn't a real bowling alley.

Everyone gasped as the pins fell, thinking it was a strike. One pin was left standing.

"Ha!" Baldur said, and in my opinion he was a little too close to Soren's face. Soren didn't have much of a temper, but I thought this might be pushing it just a tad when I saw Soren flex his fist by his side.

I stepped between the men, making sure I was facing Soren so that Baldur wouldn't get any ideas and try to kiss me.

"Let's just back it up a step guys," I said, and tried to move Soren back without pushing him.

"It was just a friendly little game. I'm sure Soren is man enough to lose at least once in his life," Baldur's voice said from behind me.

I glared over my shoulder at him.

Soren damn near growled at the other man.

"It's hard not to be a sore loser when you're being taunted by a drunken jerk," I said. I had never been fond of dealing with drunk people who couldn't control their tongue.

"I can handle losing a game," said Soren. "What I don't like is the way you stare at Helena." He pulled me in against him so tightly that I let out a little gasp of air as it was squeezed from my lungs.

I breathed him in--almost necessarily, since my face was right against his chest--as he just barely released pressure of his arm. It was enough to let me know that he had noticed his gruffness, but his stance of affronted possessiveness toward Baldur didn't change. I laid a protective, and I hoped calming, hand on his chest.

"I hope you're happy with him, Hel," Baldur said, and then I heard him walk away.

"Are you happy with me?" Soren asked, releasing his hold on me only slightly more, so I could look up into his face.

I didn't answer immediately, but tried to put some thought into it. It was hard for me to know what "happy" felt like anymore—I was always so busy just trying to survive. Not to mention the fact that anytime I thought I was really and truly happy, the rug seemed to be jerked out from underneath me.

My face felt hot and my eyes couldn't seem to stay open. Nausea hit me, and I shoved away from Soren and ran to find somewhere I could be sick without an audience.

The doors to go outside were closer than my room, and the guards opened them as they saw me running towards them.

Cold air hit my lungs, and I managed to make it to the side of the building before I collapsed. Ice cold rain soaked my dress and ran chill bumps along my skin as I laid in the dirt that was quickly turning to mud.

It felt good, though. The shock of the cold had eased my nausea and cleared my head of the awful, hot, fuzzy feeling that I had just had for the second time today. *What is wrong with me?* I asked myself, knowing I probably didn't want to know the answer.

Just like when this had happened earlier today, I was exhausted now, and this time I was too weak to go back inside.

I put my hands under my head like a pillow and fell asleep in the mud and rain.

CHAPTER
TWENTY-SIX

Someone was shaking my arm and it roused me from my nap.

I groaned, "Ugh. What do you want?" before I even saw who was trying to wake me.

"What is wrong with you? You shouldn't be sleeping out here. Your skin is ice cold," said the rich deep voice.

I opened my eyes to see Baldur standing over me. His hair was dripping wet and his shirt clung to his body. It was dark out but I almost swore I could still see those turquoise eyes.

"Hel," he said again, "are you okay?"

"I don't know," I answered him honestly. "I felt really sick, so I ran outside—then the rain was so cold and felt so good, and I was so tired..." I yawned; I was still tired.

"That doesn't sound OK," Baldur said, running his hand through his soaking wet hair again, and wiping the water out of his eyes.

He stood there staring down at me, and I knew something was wrong with me. Normally I would have gotten myself up and gone back inside, or sought out someone for help. I was sick.

"Can I help you up?" he asked me and extended a hand.

I took his hand and tried to stand in the mud that was now several inches deep around me.

I was almost to my feet when I lost my balance and fell to my knees. Baldur took hold of me underneath my arms and lifted me to my feet, like you would a child. I was standing now, with my head down to keep the rain out of my eyes while I tried to maintain my composure and balance.

My hands rested on Baldur's shoulders, and even through the wet fabric of his shirt, his body was so warm.

Chill bumps ran along my skin, and he rubbed my arms in an attempt to warm me up. Baldur was looking down into my eyes, and his face was moving closer to mine.

I knew what was happening, but I hadn't made up my mind how I felt about it. So I watched as his lips moved inch by inch towards mine.

His mouth was almost on mine. Technically, his lips might have been touching my own in the very faintest of kisses. Then my hand was on his chest, stopping him from going any further.

"I don't think I can," I said. I hadn't planned on stopping him from kissing me, and I hadn't planned on kissing him. My body had just sort of taken over my brain's decision-making process, so I went with it.

"Let's get you inside," he said, putting an arm around me to steady me as he helped me walk.

"Are you upset with me?" I asked him as we walked back to the front of the dining hall.

"Of course not, Hel. If anything, it only makes me like you more." He sighed and pulled me in a little closer against his side.

It only occurred to me once we were about to go in the front door that I really should have had Baldur take me in the back, so that everyone didn't see me. Having your queen walk through the hall, muddy and weak, wasn't a great sign of her power.

I needed some kind of doctor if this was going to keep happening. I had a feeling this wasn't some kind of underworld flu going around, and the other times I'd been ill since I died were either related to shock or vampirism.

"Do you know of a doctor I can see?" I asked Baldur.

"The Norns, maybe?"

"No. I don't ever get the feeling that they are trying to be helpful," I said simply.

He nodded, and then said, "You might not like my next answer, but he would know the most."

"Who?" I asked.

"Your father."

"Loki?"

"Yes," Baldur said, and I saw the slight curl of a smile at the edges of his lips.

"I would think you'd dread seeing him much more than me!" I laughed.

He shrugged. "I told you, there's no sense in carrying grudges like that. All of the gods try to kill each other."

"OK, I'll try to contact him tomorrow."

"I think that's a good idea."

"Running away was better than answering my question? I guess I have my answer," Soren's eyes were hot with anger when he saw Baldur and I walk in together. He obviously hadn't noticed that I was holding onto Baldur for support—or that I was shaking, and covered in mud.

"Soren, this isn't…" Baldur started, and I stopped him by tightening my grip on his arm and shaking my head.

I watched Soren turn his back on us and walk off. I could have forgiven him for not coming to check on me when I ran out earlier, but if he had only looked at me instead of Baldur in that moment, he would have seen that I was ill. I wasn't sure I could forgive him walking away like that.

Everyone else seemed to immediately realize I was not myself. Funny how jealousy could be so blinding. People kept rushing towards us and asking if I was OK, and what was wrong.

"The Queen went outside for some fresh air and slipped in the mud. She's fine, just cold and tired. Let's let her rest," Baldur reassured everyone, and helped me through the dining hall to my room.

Once we were out of earshot, I said, "Thank you for that, for all of it."

"You're welcome," he said, and helped me into my room.

"Do you want me to get Soren for you? You'll need help getting out of those wet clothes and into some dry ones—and I don't want you to be alone, since we don't know exactly what's wrong yet."

"No. I don't want to see him right now. I'll manage to get changed. I'm not quite as weak as I was."

"May I check in on you in a little while? I promise not to disturb you if you are sleeping, or if you and Soren make up." Baldur smiled.

"You may."

Baldur touched my cheek in a gentle caress. "You are my queen, and my friend. I am here for you in whatever way you might need."

I put my hand over his, holding his hand against my face. Lingering in the warmth for just a moment, knowing I wouldn't let it go any farther, even though I wanted it to.

I sighed, and let go of his hand. Watching as Baldur walked out the door, I fought every urge I had to ask him to stay.

In that second, I felt more anger towards Soren than I ever had. Not only was he not here for me when I needed him, he was here just enough to make me feel guilty for wanting to be with the man who was trying to help me.

I didn't know if I wanted him to walk through the door so I could yell at him, or if I hoped he never walked through it again.

CHAPTER
TWENTY-SEVEN

I DID MANAGE TO UNDRESS MYSELF, AND CRAWLED into bed. Sickness still weighed on my stomach, and dizziness ran through my head. There was no way I could keep trying to pretend I was OK if this didn't ease up. I just wasn't familiar enough about illness after death to know what could be making me so sick.

Chillbumps still ran along my body, so I made the fire in my room a little hotter than I normally did for sleeping, only to have to turn it down moments later when I began sweating, even though my skin was still cold to the touch.

My bed was comfortable, but I couldn't find a position that felt good. It was as though my body couldn't regulate my temperature anymore, with every little variant making me feel as though I was melting from the inside, or as though I had just come out of an ice bath.

I didn't truly feel tired, but my vision was blurring as my eyelids closed. I thought I saw someone entering the room, but couldn't tell who it was, other than that it was a woman.

A cool rag on my skin roused me from my sleep. I stretched and tried to open my eyes. I blinked and found that they were still far too heavy to keep them open.

"I can't keep my eyes open," I said to whomever was with me. Besides the press of the rag against my skin, I could feel the weight of someone on the bed. I assumed it was Soren, who had found out how ill I was.

"You don't have to try to wake up. Just rest; we've sent for help," the voice answered—only, it wasn't Soren. It was a woman's voice.

"Who went for help?" I asked.

"Baldur. He checked on you earlier and couldn't wake you, so he went to try to find Loki." I knew the voice, but was having trouble picturing her face. I hoped it was one of the women I liked.

"Oh," I said, knowing I sounded worried.

"Don't worry. I'm the only person he told how sick you are. We are keeping it from everyone else. I know you don't want to appear weak," said the woman, and I heard her wring out the rag in a tub of water.

"Thank you," I said.

"Of course, My Queen. Can I get you anything to eat or drink?" she asked.

"No, I think I'm just going to try to sleep more until he gets back. Where is Soren?" I couldn't help but ask.

"I haven't seen him in the Hall since dinner. Would you like for me to send someone to look for him?"

"No, that's alright," I told her, and rested once again. I wanted him to want to be here, and if he wasn't, I certainly didn't want him rushing to my side just because I was sick. It's not like I was able to have the conversation with him that we needed to have anyway. I didn't want him feeling guilty, and I didn't want him here.

The next time I woke up it was to a different voice in the room—one that I was happy to hear.

"How is she doing?" Baldur asked.

"She woke up once, but didn't stay awake for more than a moment," said the woman who had been looking after me.

"Did she ask for anything?"

"Nothing to eat or drink. She was worried everyone knew she was sick, and she asked where Soren was, but didn't want me to send anyone for him," the woman told him.

"I'm just happy she woke up a little," Baldur said with a sigh of relief. I could just picture him running his hands through his hair.

"Hey," I managed to speak up, and held my hand out for him.

"Hey," he said, and I felt him take my hand in his.

"Did you find Loki?" I asked.

"I wasn't able to bring him back with me—apparently there is some unrest in the underworlds again."

"Thank you," I said.

"Of course. Can I do anything for you now, or get you anything?"

"Would you stay with me awhile? Just lie with me while I rest?" I asked and squeezed his hand.

Baldur hesitated. "Are you sure you don't want me to find Soren for you?"

"I'm really sick, and the feeling isn't passing this time. I'm scared, and I don't want to fight with Soren.

I don't want to see him until I'm well."

"Let me tell the guards and the women who was here before that Soren isn't to come in here until you say so—just so we don't have to worry about the situation getting worse. Then, I will come in and stay with you," said Baldur.

I drifted back into a light sleep while Baldur took care of things going on around me. When he came back in, I roused a little when I felt him sit beside me on the edge of the bed. I opened my eyes to see him staring down at me.

"Lie down," I said, and patted the bed.

"I thought I should be on alert in case I'm needed," he said, and seemed more nervous than usual.

"I need you here."

"I'm here to serve," said Baldur and laid himself down beside me on the bed. Close, but not close enough to cuddle.

I intertwined my fingers in his once more, and knew that I was quickly falling for this man. That probably wasn't a good thing, but I didn't care.

The gentle sound of splashing water kept sleep from pulling me back in too deeply. This time it was Baldur who pressed the cool rag to my face. Chills, ran along my arms and up my neck. I wasn't sure if I was already cold, or so feverish that it made the rag feel icy.

I wrapped my hand around Baldur's thick wrist and opened my eyes. He was leaning over me, staring at me. The look in those turquoise eyes was so focused, so intense that I almost had to look away.

"I must look like death," I said.

"No, you're lovely," he said, and gave me a smile I was certain was genuine.

"Can the dead die again?" I asked.

His smile faded as he moved down in the bed, and rolled onto his side so he could face me. He seemed to be trying to think of what to say to me.

"I know that when vampires die in the mortal world, they cease to exist because their souls are gone. But the Norns put my soul back into my body. I feel like I'm dying, though. If you die and you're already dead, what else is there?" I sniffed.

Baldur touched the side of my face, and he looked worried. Before he could answer me I kept talking.

"Before I died the first time, I didn't really believe in an afterlife. I didn't want to die, but I wasn't afraid of it. I wasn't afraid of there being nothing, because how would I know? But I'm scared now—I don't want there to be nothing else after this. It's not enough," I whimpered. Tears made their way down my cheeks, and they felt cold against my hot skin. Guess that answered the fever question.

Baldur looked me dead in the eyes and said, "You are a goddess. Gods and goddesses can be killed, but they never disappear, they only transition to something or somewhere else. Even though I've only known you for a short time, I know you are brave and strong. I wouldn't worry about you anywhere. But I also know this is your destiny to rule this world, and we will not lose our queen so easily."

I managed to give him a weak smile, and said, "I hope you're right."

"Rest, Queen Hel. I won't leave you," said Baldur.

I moved closer to him, so that he could wrap his arms around me, protect me, hold me. Then I slowly drifted back into sleep.

CHAPTER
TWENTY-EIGHT

"ISN'T THIS COZY-LOOKING?" LOKI'S VOICE SANG IN through my bedroom.

It was obvious he was trying to be loud enough to wake us.

Baldur untangled himself from my arms just enough to sit up, taking my hand to his lips and kissing it when I tried to hold onto him.

"Wake up. He's here," he said to me.

I tried to rouse myself from my sleepy daze, and Baldur helped me to sit up. I was sitting up in bed, but all of my strength was gone, even more so than before I laid down earlier. My full weight was leaned back against my headboard. This was so not good.

"You look a little pale, daughter," Loki said after he walked over to me and leaned in, nearly nose to nose.

"Do you know what's wrong with me?" I asked. "I feel like I'm dying."

"You are," said Loki in his oh-so-casual way.

"What is it? How do we cure her?" Baldur asked before I could manage to.

"I thought you of all people would recognize poisoning, Baldur," Loki said with a sly smile.

"Punch him," I breathed softly to Baldur.

Both men ignored my statement, but I was serious.

"What kind of poison?" I asked, after a moment of summoning the strength to speak.

"Eitr," Loki answered as he plopped himself back down in the chair near my bed.

"Eitr?" Baldur said, and gripped my hand so tightly I almost needed him to back off. "There's no cure for that."

"Afraid not. It's going to kill you," Loki looked right at me as he said the words.

I took as deep a breath as I could manage. This was it: of all the things I had lost and endured, it was going to end here.

"I thought you told her she had some great purpose to serve here! The Norns dragged her here against her will just so she could be poisoned and die?" Baldur roared at Loki. "She's your daughter, for god's sake. Do something!"

"I'm afraid there's really nothing I can do to stop the poison coursing through her being. You know how this goes Baldur, living in the world of the gods. Nothing is ever for certain."

"I need to send a message to Grace, and Boude, and Andreas. They need to know that I love them," I whispered, trying not to cry. I knew I didn't have much time left, and I needed to put things in order.

"Do you know who has poisoned her? If we can't save her, at least help me avenge her!" Baldur was still on the rampage.

Loki started to speak, but I held up my hand. "No. I don't want to know who has done this to me. I don't want to spend my last remaining time angry.

163

Send someone to find Soren for me—he deserves a goodbye… And bring me Garmr."

Baldur reluctantly let go of my hand and went to the door. I heard him speaking to someone, and then he came back to my side.

I looked at Loki and asked, "Is there anything else, beyond this, when I die this time? Do I go to some other level of death? Where does it stop?"

Loki shrugged and said, "Eitr is the poison of all poisons: the only thing strong enough to kill a god or goddess of our power. I can't say what you will see or where you will go, if there is anything at all."

"Do I need to choose someone to lead Helheim after I am gone?" I asked, still trying to be reasonable.

"No, you've done such an excellent job as queen, I'm sure the people will stand for nothing less than suitable." Loki smiled and looked almost proud.

"Yeah, such a great job I got myself poisoned within no time of ruling." I rolled my eyes. "I still don't want to know who, but I would like to know why. Did I do something wrong? Was I unfair or cruel to someone to make them want to kill me?" I asked.

"My child, life and death have more mysteries than we can ever solve," said Loki.

"Are the children alright? Has Caireen taken them yet?" I asked as the thought occurred to me.

"Yes, they are gone. Everything and everyone is doing fine," Baldur reassured me. At least that was a relief.

Someone knocked at the door and Baldur moved away from me. "Come in," he said.

The door opened and Garmr bounded into the room and onto my bed. He snuggled up beside me, the size of a grown man. He placed his giant head on my leg, and I put my hand on it. He knew.

Then one of the guards poked his head in. "Soren is here to see The Queen. Shall I send him in?"

"Give us just a moment," said Baldur, then he turned to me. "I'll leave the two of you alone, and if you want me to come back, just call for William. He'll be standing by the door."

"Thank you," I told him.

Baldur headed for the door, but Loki stayed in his chair. I looked at him, seeing if he would get the hint, but finally had to say, "Can you excuse us too?"

"Oh, sorry. Of course," he said, and pushed himself up from the chair to follow Baldur out the door.

Soren came in as my two visitors were leaving. The look he gave Baldur was meant to be hateful and sharp, but when he saw Loki it faded into confusion. Then, he saw me.

"Are you OK?" he asked, but didn't move any closer. I wasn't sure if he thought I was contagious, or faking.

"No. I'm not. Soren, can you come a little closer? It's hard for me to speak very loudly."

Soren walked to my side and stood there looking down at me. He was concerned, and I knew he cared for me—but we had taken a very wrong turn somewhere, because he just didn't look at me the same as he used to. In a way, that hurt more than knowing that I was dying.

"Soren, before I tell you this, promise me you won't get angry. I don't need drama right now. I just need you to know something, and give some people messages for me. OK?" I pleaded.

"I'll do my best," he said reluctantly.

"Someone has poisoned me with Eitr. I'm dying—again—and I don't think there's anything left for me after here..." Those were all of the words I got out before Soren moved into my bed and pulled me into his arms.

"No," he repeated over and over as he started crying into my hair.

"Soren, listen. I need you to let Grace know what happened, and that I love her. Please tell her to give the same message to Andreas and Boude," I told him and then leaned back against his warm, big body that had held me so many times. I turned in his arms so that I could see his face and said, "You know I love you, too. Even when I've been angry with you, or haven't wanted to see you. I love you."

"Helena, I'm so sorry I was angry over Baldur. I can't believe I stormed away from you. I had no idea," he sobbed.

"Shh," I said, pressing a finger to his lips. "It's no time for guilt or anger. Kiss me please."

Soren shifted our bodies so that I was in his lap, and he was holding me almost like you would hold a baby. He kissed me, a firm but gentle press of his lips to mine.

It was sweet and perfect, and as I relaxed into the feel of resting in his arms, I realized I was no longer burning up or freezing. I felt just right.

CHAPTER
TWENTY-NINE

I OPENED MY EYES, AND THINGS WERE CLEAR. MY eyelids no longer felt heavy, and my body felt good. Looking up, I realized I wasn't in my bedroom. The sky was a cloudy blue-gray, and I could see trees. I was still in Helheim. I guess I hadn't died after all.

I smiled, wondering who had cured me of the incurable poison, and thinking of the sweet kiss Soren and I had shared. That kiss was the last thing that I remembered, and I wanted to repeat it immediately.

Carefully, I sat up to try to figure out exactly where someone had taken me. I was up high on some kind of scaffold-like stand, and when I looked down, I saw I had been dressed in my elegant black dress—the one I had worn on my night out with Soren.

I was on soft bedding, but the platform I was on was made of wood. The smell of woodsmoke was strong in the air. Initially it offered comfort, let me know someone was close by—until I realized that what was burning was the wooden structure beneath me. *Shit, shit, shit.*

Smoke started rolling up around the sides of my bed, making it difficult for me to see any direction but up. It was definitely too high for me to consider jumping down. Through the smoke, I thought I saw the shadows of people walking away. *Why would they burn me and leave? Is it because the poison hadn't worked? Are they that determined to kill me?* "Help!" I called out. "Please, someone help me!"

I heard the crackling of the fire as it crept it's way up towards me—I heard the popping of the wood as the flames consumed it faster and faster. I wondered if the pyre would fall or burn up first. I wondered if the flames would reach me before the smoke could render me unconscious. None of these options were looking good; jumping was my only real choice to avoid the smoke and flames. But I didn't know what kind of injury that would cause, either. Two broken legs would be better than feeling my skin melt off, though.

I called out for help a few more times, until the black smoke filled my lungs and I couldn't scream without coughing.

Ray had told me as a child that there are safe ways to fall from high places. Stunt men and people trained to fight know how to move in the air and land so that they don't get injured—just like cats almost always land on their feet. It was nice to know there was a way to do it safely. It would have been better if I had known what that safe way was.

Closing my eyes, I stepped to the edge of the platform and imagined I was about to dive into a large, beautiful swimming pool. Right at that moment I was swept back into a memory of Hell, and my psyche tried to tell me that no, it wasn't a relaxing dip in the pool, but that we were jumping into the lake of fire that I had so narrowly escaped the first time.

There was no one here to save me now—no demons to drag me away to an even worse fate, no Raphael to rescue me, no Loki to pop in as my protector. Just flames and smoke, and no choice but to jump anyway.

The first lick of flames reached the top, and I jumped. Only I didn't fall very far before I landed with a soft thump on a terrain I didn't recognize as dirt or grass. It was shaped like a firm hill, and covered in cloth. The hill moved, and I realized where I had landed only moments before the giant spoke.

"Hello, Queen Hel," said Hugi.

"I am so happy to see you!" I laughed, and patted his shoulder. "What are you doing here?"

"Baldur told me to watch over you. To make sure no one tried to take your body."

My arms were shaking as I took in the information and tried to hold on to the moving giant. "Did Baldur set the fire that was supposed to burn me?"

"Him and a few other people," Hugi said.

"They wanted me dead?" I asked, half to myself and half to Hugi. Then I realized he was walking me closer to town.

"Nooo," the giant dragged out the word as if that was such a ridiculous thought. "You were already dead, have been for several days."

"Oh," I said. "How did I come back then?"

"I don't know. Maybe it had something to do with that guy who kept sneaking out here and putting drops of stuff in your mouth," he mused.

"Did he look kind of out of place? Short reddish hair, clean cut?" I asked.

"Yeah, that's why he stood out to me so much," Hugi answered.

"That's Loki, my father."

"Hm. I thought he would be taller."

I chuckled at the giant's musing, and let him carry me back to town. I didn't have to wonder how he had gotten in the gates of Helheim. I knew that Baldur must have let him in, and while I wasn't terribly happy about him setting me on fire, I could forgive him since he thought I was dead.

Everyone was in for a very big surprise—everyone except Loki, of course.

CHAPTER THIRTY

I MADE HUGI PUT ME DOWN JUST BEFORE WE TOPPED the hill. I didn't want anyone focusing more on there being a giant in town than on my return.

I thanked him profusely and hugged him again, as much as I could manage. He smiled at me, and even blushed a little.

Still wearing the black evening gown, and barefoot, I walked through the velvety grass. When I reached the top of the hill, I looked into town—into my world, my creation.

It made me so happy to see everyone doing their daily tasks. Maybe it was just wishful thinking, but it seemed that the town had taken on a bit of a somber mood with their belief that I had died. People weren't moving quite as fast, and no one had a smile as big as they normally did. I wondered if my supposed passing had really bothered them this much.

A hand gripped my shoulder from behind and I gasped, too frightened to even scream. I whipped around to see who had me, terrified that I was about to be dragged away again to be killed.

"It's just me," Loki said, leaning forward on me,

breathing heavily, like he had been running for ages.

"What the hell?" I demanded.

"Sorry… Didn't…. Know…. Baldur…. Was setting the fire today," he told me in gasps. "Once I found out, I ran out there to get you, but you were gone. Then I saw the giant heading towards town, and it's very hard to follow a giant."

I smiled at him, and asked, "How did you bring me back?"

"Eitr," he grinned, and in that grin was every bit of mischief the stories told of him.

"Eitr is what killed me," I said.

"It is both a giver of life and a deadly poison. There was no cure for it once it had taken hold of your system, but once you were dead, it was the only way to bring you back."

"Did you know that all along?" I asked, feeling a little less grateful now.

"Of course, otherwise I would have never poisoned you to begin with."

"What! You are the one who poisoned me?" I yelled.

"Sorry, I couldn't have you knowing. You would have wanted to reassure Baldur and Soren, and I couldn't have that. Your death had to be real," he said.

"It was still real!"

"Yes, but I knew I was bringing you back."

"But I didn't!" It felt completely pointless to argue with him. I rubbed my temples. "So what was the point in killing me and bringing me back?"

"See," he said, "now that is a good question. Now you are immortal even beyond the level of a normal goddess. You have strength and power over life and death like no one before you."

"If dying by Eitr and being brought back by it gives you immortality, then why don't all the gods do that?" I asked.

"Do you really think we would trust one another to bring us back?"

"Good point," I said.

"Besides, it would only really work for you. You were born with power over death—over the grave. Most other gods can't touch death in the way that you can. Since Eitr is a bringer of life and death, it was suited to you," he told me.

"OK, but why did I need to go through this? I already had powers, why did I need to die to get more?" I asked.

"My sweet, raised by a mortal, girl. More power is always better—and I've heard rumors of a war coming between the underworlds. Nothing I can share yet, but I wanted us to be ahead of the game."

"A war?" I asked, feeling my stomach tighten.

Loki waved his hand as if that would wave away my concern. "Come along, let's get you back to your people."

Loki announced my return (leaving out his role in the whole situation, of course), and told a brilliant story of how the person who had poisoned me had been dealt with swiftly. Obviously I was meant to be ruler of Helheim, Queen of Death, Queen over the Grave.

People gasped when they saw me, and knelt down before me—kneeling, seeing themselves as less than me... seeing me as someone worthy of being honored in such a way. It was never the role I wanted, but whenever I tried to tell them to please stand, Loki gave me a cutting look that said to leave well enough alone.

Soon I was swept up in a sea of the townspeople, being carried on their shoulders to the hall amidst cheers and chants and laughter. I was so stunned at everything that had happened, I just couldn't seem to take it all in.

On hearing the chaos, the hall doors opened and Baldur stepped out, a look of disbelief on his face as he rubbed his eyes and blinked at me. I smiled and gave him a small wave from atop my chariot of hands and shoulders.

He grinned and joined the crowd in their cheering.

In all of the movement, a statue-still pair of icy gray eyes caught my attention. My Viking. Soren saw me, but didn't smile. He made no move to come towards me or celebrate my return. He watched from the side of the hall as I was carried in, and he didn't follow.

Tears burned my eyes as I thought of that last kiss we shared. My heart suddenly hurt so much that I thought I might collapse if they weren't carrying me. Why wasn't he glad that I was back?

Everyone placed me gently on the ground and began asking me questions about my death and planning a big celebration. Garmr greeted me with wet kisses and a wagging tail that could double as a lethally effective whip.

I fake-smiled and tried to make my way to the doors, out to Soren. This couldn't wait.

Loki stopped me at the door with a hand on my shoulder. "Where do you think you are going?" he asked.

"I have to talk to Soren," I said as I tried to push past him.

"No, he is not important right now. You are. Your people need you. You have to be part of their celebration. You are a goddess—a Queen of Death—not a goddess who chases moody Vikings."

"I understand, and I'll be right back. But if you don't let me take care of this, I won't be able to pretend anything for long, and they will definitely notice," I argued.

Loki rolled his eyes and stepped aside so I could pass.

As I was going outside I heard him announce, "Our Queen has quick business to attend to before joining our party! Carry on!"

I followed the sound of hammer striking metal, and made my way the short distance to the forge that I didn't even know had been built. I watched as Soren struck a piece of iron over and over, stopping once to wipe the sweat from his brow.

"What are you making?" I asked softly.

"Horseshoes," he said, in a tone that matched my own. He wouldn't look at me.

My chest was hurting so much, and I was biting my lower lip trying to keep the tears back. He didn't say anything to me, and I didn't know what to say to him.

You are not a goddess who chases moody Vikings, Loki's voice rang in my head. I took a deep breath and walked over to Soren, standing in front of him so that he had to see me.

I forced myself to stand up straight and keep eye contact. I was a goddamn queen now. Even with all of our history and how much we had loved each other, I didn't want to waste anymore time trying to figure out what I had done wrong.

"I can tell that we're done," I said, and swallowed hard. "I'd like to know why, though."

Soren's eyes softened as he looked me over. "You're not Helena anymore. You don't even look like my Helena. You're not the simple gravedigger who wanted a simple life with me," he said.

Anger flared in my cheeks. "Soren, I've told you. If I could give all of this up and go back to digging up souls with you and Billy—or even digging graves back in my cemetery—I'd throw all of this away in a second. This isn't what I want! I'm just trying to make the best of it. I thought you understood that. I haven't changed, I've adapted."

Soren dropped his gaze from mine and I could tell there was something else he wanted to say.

"What is this really about?" I asked.

"What I said is true, we're just not a good match for each other anymore. You might want a simple life, but that's not what you're going to get, and… fuck, Helena, I can't keep losing you—can't keep watching you leave or die, and never knowing when it's the end. I'm glad you are OK this time, but I've said goodbye to you too many times, and I can't keep doing it. I hope you understand that."

"I don't. I've said goodbye to you the same amount of times that you've said goodbye to me. I still want to make things work with you," I said.

He shook his head, all emotions aside from frustration were gone. "I don't. I don't want every day with you as queen to be a new death threat or drama. I don't want to help rule over an entire underworld and make sure everyone is cared for. I want it to be just us, no more dying, no more vampires or zombies, or shit to deal with. Can you give me that?"

I answered him simply with a single word, "No."

CHAPTER
THIRTY-ONE

I MADE IT THROUGH THE FESTIVITIES IN MY HONOR with a smile on my face. My heart was hurt, but I had told Loki that I just needed things settled between Soren and myself, and they were.

I didn't even have time to go to my room and change or put on a pair of shoes. God knows what I probably looked like after being dead. People stared at me and touched my hair to see if I was indeed really there, but I was shown nothing but love. It helped, a little.

The party continued until people were falling asleep or passing out on the tables, and when I laid my head down on my crossed arms, a gentle nudge kept me from closing my eyes.

"The Queen shouldn't be sleeping on a hard table," Baldur's deep, gentle voice whispered to me.

"The Queen is too tired to walk," I said with half closed eyes.

"The Queen speaking in third person is also a bad sign," he said with a grin. Baldur took my hand in his and helped me stand. I had been around him for short periods of time during the party, but everyone was huddled around me so that we couldn't have said more than ten words to one another.

"I'm sorry I set you on fire today," he said sheepishly.

I rubbed the tiredness from my eyes and laughed. "It's not like you knew I was coming back," I said. "Luckily you had let Hugi into Helheim. He rescued me."

Baldur smiled, "He's a good giant."

We walked quietly for a time, and then Baldur asked, "So, was there anything after this?"

I shook my head, trying to think. "I remember Soren kissing me, and then I woke up on the pyre." I shrugged, then stopped. Faint images of giant black wings were far in the back of my mind, a kind voice, but none of it was clear enough to warrant mentioning. My mind was probably just trying to fill in the gaps.

"I noticed Soren wasn't around this evening," said Baldur.

"Yep. Apparently having your girlfriend be a goddess of death makes things a little too complicated," I told him. My voice was bitter, and I didn't care.

Baldur put his hand on my shoulder, it wasn't flirty though, just sympathetic. "I'm sorry," he said.

"He's probably right. He wants a simple existence, and who would want to be with someone who was constantly finding new ways to die, along with being brought into every type of underworld drama imaginable?"

"Someone who knows who you are and what greatness you are capable of. Someone who thinks it's an honor to be in your presence day after day for as long as they get to have you," Baldur said, with a look that was so intense I looked away. I couldn't do this right now.

We were just outside my bedroom door, and of course he stepped forward to open it for me. I looked into the room, and couldn't bring myself to go in.

I stood in the doorway shaking my head.

"What's wrong?" Baldur asked.

"I can't sleep in there. I died in that bed, in Soren's arms, and I just can't," I told him, as tears spilled down my cheeks.

Baldur put an arm around me and pulled me back as he closed the door. "Where can I take you?"

"I don't know," I said with a sigh, and looked down at the floor trying to think. "I want out of this damn dress and I need some shoes." I knew I didn't have the energy or strength to try to conjure myself clothes right now.

"OK, do you want me to go in there and get you something else to wear and some shoes? Then we can decide where you want to stay."

I nodded. "Please."

I leaned against the wall while Baldur went back into my room. I expected it to take him a little while to find my things, but he emerged in just a moment holding nearly all of the clothes I had in my room and two pairs of boots.

"Where do you want me to take you?" he asked again.

"There are a few empty rooms farther down the hallway, I think," I told him. "Any of those should be fine."

My voice didn't sound like things were fine, though; everything that had happened was slowly sinking in. The numbness of my death, my resurrection, and then my broken heart—it was all wearing off, and it hurt.

We walked a long way down the hallway and he opened one of the doors. The room was chilly and plain. Baldur immediately put my clothes down and started building me a fire in the small fireplace. I almost stopped him, since I knew I could make one with just a thought, but I didn't. I didn't even feel as though I had the energy to think a fire into existence.

"Thank you," I said.

"Of course. What else do you need?" he asked.

"I, uh... I need help out of this dress," I said, and turned around so that he could help with the zipper that was just out of reach.

Baldur cleared his throat and acted slightly uncomfortable, but said, "Oh, sure, I can do that."

His warm fingers brushed against my skin and I remembered Soren helping me out of this dress the last time I wore it. I had felt so beautiful that night, and even though the Norns had pretty much messed everything up, it was still a special night. I did not feel beautiful now, and I wanted this fucking dress off and far away from me.

The zipper was stuck, and I felt Baldur trying to free the caught material. "Just break it, or tear it if you need to," I told him.

"I think I can get it loose," he said.

I looked up as he worked with the dress and saw a mirror over the fireplace. I hadn't even looked at myself since I had woken up, and what I saw scared the hell out of me. One of my eyes was white, and on the same side of my body my hair had turned black. I looked as though I was half dead.

I gasped, covering my mouth, and stepped back so suddenly that I fell into Baldur and took him down with me. Any embarrassment or mild injury from the fall was overtaken by my sobs.

"What?! What happened?" asked Baldur.

"Why didn't anyone tell me I'm hideous?!" I cried. "*Of course* Soren didn't want me and everyone has been looking at me so weird. I'm a monster."

Baldur sat up and made me look at him, holding my face between his hands. "Have I looked at you weird this evening?"

I thought about it: when he initially saw me, he'd stared a moment longer than usual, but that was just surprise. Not once this evening had he cringed or treated me differently. "No," I said.

"You are far from a monster, and if Soren's feelings changed because you look a little different, I'll think much less of him as a man." Baldur smiled at me. "This might even wear off, but even if it doesn't, you are still as beautiful as ever.. Dying is bound to come with some side effects. Don't be disheartened. Your people still love you, and I..." he stopped.

My heart beat a little faster, and I blinked the last few tears from my eyes letting them roll down my cheeks. "You what?" I asked.

"I might be in love with you," he said, wiping a tear from my face with his thumb.

My brain tried to send off some alarm bells, more about my own choices than anything to do with Baldur; but the bells were soft, and I wasn't listening anyway. I looked at his rich turquoise eyes and that beautiful golden skin. My eyes dipped down to his full lips—and then, those lips were on mine.

Baldur's kisses were passionate, but still so gentle, just like his touch. Even at Soren's easiest, there was still pressure—a little bit of power and force behind his caresses.

Baldur's tongue explored my mouth, and I pressed my body against his. I raked my nails gently down the side of his neck and dug my fingers into his shoulders as I tried to turn so that I was no longer just being held by him, but facing him on his lap.

The material from my dress was bunched beneath me, keeping me from being able to feel everything that I wanted to feel. I tugged at the bodice, trying to see if Baldur had ever managed to dislodge the broken zipper. It still didn't budge.

I broke our kiss to say, "Get this thing off of me."

I turned around so that Baldur could resume his task of getting me out of this dress: this dress that had been my funeral dress, this dress that I had worn on my special date with Soren. I was letting another man help me out of the dress that Soren had been the last one to take off of me. We only broke up earlier today. *Shouldn't I feel bad about that? Am I just trying to numb myself again?*

"I'm afraid I can't get it unstuck without breaking the zipper," Baldur said.

"Then break it," I told him.

I felt the force of the metal teeth being torn apart by Baldur's hands, and it brought a rush of heat to my face. There was just something about a man tearing your clothes off of you that was a huge turn on. Even though it's not that hard to break a zipper, it was still hot.

Once I felt the fabric part down to my hips, I sighed. Baldur slipped his hands beneath the fabric and wrapped them around my bare waist. I shivered and leaned back against him.

His large warm hands kneaded my sides, down to my hips, and then slowly made their way up to cup my breasts, still being painstakingly gentle with his touches.

"I won't break," I breathed, laying my head back against his shoulder.

"There are times to be firm," he said, jerking my hips back against his so that I could feel his own firmness pressed against my ass, even through the dress. The motion brought a gasp from my lips. "And there are times to be gentle, to let the desire build until it's almost unbearable," he continued, planting a kiss on my neck so light that it was like the whisper of a breeze on my skin.

I turned in his arms and kissed him again, letting my fingers play in that silken hair that looked like it had been kissed by the sunshine. Kissing him was like tasting sunshine, so bright and refreshing—like I had been in the dark for ages.

He grabbed the sides of my dress and helped pull the tightest part past my hips so that the rest of it could fall to the floor. I could tell women had dressed me after my death. The dress didn't need a bra, and I wasn't wearing one, but I was wearing panties. Most men would have dressed me without any under-clothes at all, or put a bra on me even though the dress was a corset-style bodice.

The open air of the room immediately poured over me, and I pressed myself against Baldur even harder.

Baldur tore his lips away from mine, kissed a line down my neck, and continued kneeling down until he was level with my breasts. I sighed with pleasure and placed my hands on his shoulders to steady myself.

Movement caught my eye and I looked up into the mirror to see a stranger watching us—only it wasn't a stranger. That dark hair and milky eye belonged to me; the skin on that side wasn't tan like a girl who had spent her life working outside. It was so white it was nearly gray, and I could see the lines of the blue veins beneath the skin. The reflection reminded me of the vampire Rasputin who had tried to kill me. The thought made my stomach turn, and even the feel of Baldur's tongue and teeth on my nipple wasn't enough to distract me.

The woman looking at us in the mirror couldn't be a part of me—this couldn't be what I looked like now... but it was.

"Stop," I said, with a gentle push on Baldur's shoulders.

"What's wrong?" He looked up at me.

"I just can't do this. I've always used sex as a way to stop feeling the bad things, and to make myself feel something good, but it's not fair for me to use you this way," I told him.

"You didn't mind using me this way a few minutes ago. It's the way you look, isn't it?" he asked.

"How can you kiss me, touch me, when I'm so disgusting?" I covered my face with my hands and closed my eyes.

Baldur grabbed my hands and pulled them away from my face. He turned me so that I couldn't see myself in the mirror and said, "Hel, look at me."

I opened my eyes a bit and glanced up at him.

"No, really look at me."

I did.

"You are still you. So, parts of you look a little

different. I still see the gorgeous, vibrant blonde that I startled, naked, in the pool when we met," he told me, touching the *dead* side of my face. "This is like a scar: it shows you've been all the way to the end of the road and back. I'm not sure anyone else, god or goddess, has managed that." He ran his fingers through my black hair, "This is your badge of honor. I will never think that isn't beautiful—that you aren't beautiful."

I looked into Baldur's face. His perfect face, with those eyes that could nearly glow in the dark, his golden skin... Maybe he was right, maybe it was supposed to be my badge of honor. It still didn't feel like one though.

"Hel, we can get in bed, and I can watch over you, hold you while you rest. I can leave you alone, or I can make love to you." Baldur used the back of his hand to trace a gentle line down my breast. "You say the word."

"I don't think I'm in the right mindset for sex right now. Not that I don't want to, just that I want to be completely consumed by desire when I share that with you. It's not fair to either of us if I'm not all in," I explained. I still couldn't believe those words were coming out of my mouth.

Baldur looked serious, but not angry. "Do you want me to go?"

I shook my head. "No, please stay with me."

He smiled then and wrapped his arms around me, holding me in a hug that I sank into, and I finally felt like I could breathe for the first time today.

We climbed into bed and I laid my head on Baldur's chest, my leg draped over his legs and my fingers gently playing with his hair.

He held me and gently stroked my back and hair until I was in that fuzzy point between sleep and wakefulness. I fidgeted more than I wanted to, and sighed in frustration.

"What's wrong?" he asked.

"I'm afraid to go to sleep," I told him.

"Why?"

"What if I don't wake up again?" I asked, wondering if he was going to laugh at me.

"You're not dying again, it's only sleep. I've got you, and I promise you will wake up," he assured me.

I nodded, and closed my eyes.

CHAPTER
THIRTY-TWO

BLACK WINGS. BLACK WINGS THAT SPANNED FIFTEEN feet across, at least. The wings seemed to be in the spotlight, shadowed so that I couldn't see the face of the one who owned those majestic wings.

"I just came to check on you." Those words ran through my head, and I wasn't sure if it was a thought I was having or if that was how he was speaking to me.

I thought back at him, "I'm back, but other than that I'm not sure." I was curious to see if I received an answer.

"Are you happy I brought you back?" followed my own thought.

I immediately responded with, "Of course!" But then, I added, "I think."

The black wings drooped a bit, as if he was disappointed. They made a whooshing sound as they sank.

"Don't take it the wrong way. I am happy to be here. I just lost a lot today, and even with everything I have, it still hurts."

"I'm sorry about Soren," was the next thought from him.

I sniffled and said, "Thanks. So, was it you who brought me back, or the eitr that Loki gave me?"

"It was the eitr that summoned me."

I nodded: that made sense. "Are you an angel?"

"I am."

"Does that mean you're a servant of the Christian God?" I asked.

"Something like that," he said.

"Why did you bring me back?"

"Because you needed to be saved, and I owed you."

"You owed me? Do I know you?" I asked, completely puzzled.

I couldn't see the angel's expression but I felt him smile.

"That's not important."

I touched the side of my face and pulled a piece of dark hair over my shoulder. "Will I look like this from now on?"

"Are you unhappy with your appearance?"

"I just don't feel like I'm me anymore," I sighed, feeling selfish. "I'm sorry—you saved me, and it could be so much worse. I don't mean to sound ungrateful."

"The mark of death will serve you in the coming days."

Chill bumps prickled my skin as his words rolled through my head. "What does that mean?"

"If you need anything, simply ask."

"What's your name?" I asked quickly because I could feel his presence fading.

Another smile washed over me and he was gone.

My eyes opened and I yawned. I was still wrapped around Baldur, but felt another weight and warmth at my back. I turned my head to see Garmr snuggled up beside me. I smiled at the dog, and then at Baldur.

"He insisted on coming in, and I thought he was going to break the door down," he laughed.

"I'm glad," I told him.

"How did you sleep?" he asked.

"I think I slept OK. Do you know anything about angels?"

"Angels?" Baldur repeated, with a puzzled look on his face. "Very little. Why?"

"I think it was an angel that brought me back. I think something big is coming. Loki said something along those lines as well."

"Where there is power there can never truly be peace," Baldur said. "Should we be preparing for whatever might be on its way?"

"How do you prepare if you don't know what you'll be fighting?" I asked him.

"You train your people, get plans in place for anything you can think might happen. Have your warriors ready for physical battle, and your wise men and women ready for spiritual battles and negotiations."

"You've got way more experience in these things than I do," I told him.

"My experience is at your service any time that you need me." He planted a gentle kiss on my head.

"Could you do that for me? Take care of making the plans and getting everyone prepared in case something is on the way?"

"Of course."

"All I ask is that once you have these plans in place, you explain them to me, and your reasoning for them. I want to learn. If I'm going to be a good queen, I need to understand warfare and preparation." I looked him in the eyes so he could see this was important to me.

"And the fact that you want to know these things shows that you are already a good queen. I'll begin speaking with people today to see what roles can be filled," he said, and I could already see the wheels turning in his mind.

"Do you want me to include Soren in these plans?" Baldur asked.

"If he wants to participate," I answered.

"Of course."

I covered my face with my arm and sighed.

"What is it? What's troubling you now?" Baldur asked.

"I just don't know what my next step is? I just died, and came back. I can't even look at myself in the mirror right now, and even though everyone keeps telling me how powerful I am... I feel powerless."

"My Queen, you are not powerless. However you are ill-trained for your position."

I rolled my eyes at him and said, "Gee thanks."

"Were you good at digging graves when you first started?" he asked.

"I started digging as a small child. I'm sure I wasn't any good at it, but I don't really remember learning how to do it."

"Tell me, how do you choose a plot, dig a grave? What is the process?" Baldur asked.

"That's not a relevant skill here."

"No, but indulge me."

"You have to know the land, and the seasons. Is the ground rocky, are there tree roots under the soil? How big the plot needs to be, and if they are wanting to save room for someone else to be near them, like a spouse."

"And why is it important to know these things?"

"So you can choose the right tools," I said, and in my mind I was back in the rolling hills of my cemetery with the creaky gate.

"Right. Leading a country—or, as it were, an underworld—is no different. You have to learn the land, your weaknesses, the people in and around your territory. Know their strengths and weaknesses, so that you have the physical and mental tools to deal with whatever situation you are faced with."

"A cemetery of a few acres of dead people is not the same as an underworld, or a war. There's way more to it," I argued.

"That's why you need help. You wouldn't know all that you know without Ray teaching you, and learning from your mistakes. Once you have the tools in place, this will be no different."

"The difference is I wanted that graveyard, I loved what I did there. I chose to learn and stay there. I didn't choose this."

Baldur stared back into my eyes as intensely as I had ever seen. I thought he was angry with me for wallowing in self-pity. We both knew I couldn't go back to that life, and it was pointless to still be longing for it as I was. I couldn't blame him for being frustrated with me. I was frustrated with myself, and he had done nothing but try to help.

It was only once his lips were against mine that I realized I had misread the look I had seen on his face.

I let him kiss me; even though I didn't move to take things further, I didn't pull away. I reveled in the flavor of him, tasting his sweet and salty mouth as he tasted mine.

After a time, he pulled away and I felt his body shudder. His forehead was pressed to mine, and his eyes were closed. "I have never had a woman make me feel so strong, and so weak at the same time. You make me feel both hopeful, and helpless."

I closed my eyes and brought my hands up from my sides to place them on his shoulders.

Hot tears spilled down my cheeks. "I'm sorry," I breathed with my lips almost against his.

"No, do not be sorry. Just as you need to learn to be hard at times, I need to learn to be softer."

I knew he was referring to an emotional kind of soft, but at the moment, with his body pressed against me, there was absolutely nothing soft about it.

"I have never wanted anyone the way that I want you," he told me.

"My body wants you as much you want me, but my heart isn't capable of making a connection right now. I don't know if it ever will be. It's been broken too many times."

"You're saying you don't know if you can ever love me?"

"Yes, that's what I'm saying."

"Do you still love Soren?"

"I remember what it felt like to love him, and I'm still sad and hurt by his actions. But no, I don't feel what I remember as love."

"Hel. I'm not asking for your love, or trying to win your heart. Right now, I'm asking you to share your body with me. To take me inside of you and allow me to give you an escape from this darkness you are so lost in. I want to serve you, because you are my queen."

I stared up into his intense, stunning gaze, and realized exactly what he was offering… and how much I wanted it.

CHAPTER
THIRTY-THREE

I PULLED BALDUR BACK DOWN TO ME AS I RAISED my head to kiss him. This time I didn't hold back. He never took his lips from mine as he got rid of the bits of blanket and clothing that separated our bodies. I wrapped my legs around his waist, and there was no hesitation as he pushed himself inside of me.

The feeling of him so deep in me filled a need I didn't know that I had. My hips moved frantically against his, even though he was trying to exert a little control and last as long as possible.

He groaned against my mouth as my hips did most of the work from the bottom. "If you keep that up, I won't last," he said, and sounded almost afraid.

"I'm so close," I told him. "Just wait for me."

He growled and buried his face against my neck. "Hel, what are you doing to me?" His voice was thick and strained.

"I need you," I said, and although my orgasm was so close, my hips were starting to give out.

Baldur made a fist with my hair in his hand, and I gasped as he began matching the pace that I had started. I cried out and found myself back at that edge, aching to throw myself over.

I wrapped my legs around him even tighter and felt myself begin to fall into that place of pleasure, of nothingness.

I screamed against his neck and dug my fingers into his shoulders as my body spasmed around his, causing him fall into his own release. He collapsed on top of me, and we stayed that way for a long time, just breathing and holding one another.

When I was finally able to speak, all I could think to say was, "Thank you."

Baldur blinked those gorgeous turquoise eyes at me and said, "Happy to serve you, My Queen."

I wasn't thinking about my new appearance, or wondering if I'd ever love again, but I felt energized—and underneath that, I felt angry. I was tired of losing, of having what I loved snatched from beneath me. I was ready to learn how to fight, how to plan, and how to rule. If it was in my power to prevent that pain of loss from happening again, I would do everything within my power as a goddess to create the future I wanted—and I was ready to kill for it.

Baldur saw the far-away intensity in my eyes as I stared at nothing, and asked, "What do you want to do now?"

"Teach me to fight," I commanded. My voice was flat and level, and I realized that this must have always been my path—my destiny. "Teach me how to be a warrior. Teach me how to be a Ruler of the Dead—a Queen of the Grave."

THE STORY WILL CONTINUE...

Want to be the first to have a sneak peek at my new books, giveaways, and free Kindle downloads?

JOIN MY MAILING LIST!

https://mailchi.mp/fa5e03851766/williedalton

ABOUT THE AUTHOR

WILLIE E. DALTON writes in her beautiful home in Pound, VA. She is the author of *Three Witches in a Small Town, The Dark Side of the Woods,* and *The Gravedigger series.* When she isn't writing, Willie enjoys spending time with her daughter, reading, and volunteering with the local cat rescue.

To learn more about Willie and her books, go to:

WWW.AUTHORWILLIEDALTON.COM

WWW.FACEBOOK.COM/AUTHORWILLIEDALTON
WWW.INSTAGRAM.COM/AUTHORWILLIEDALTON